The Chocolate Comeback

The Chocolate Comeback

A Love at the Chocolate Shop Romance

Roxanne Snopek

TULE
PUBLISHING

Dedication

To Ray, who always believes in me

Acknowledgments

With gratitude to CJ Carmichael, who provided the perfect ending to this story, editor Sinclair Sawhney, whose suggestions are always bang on and the amazing Tule angels, who make it all happen.

A huge thank you to my friend, author Paula Altenburg, who reads and comments so generously and can somehow make sense of my plots, when they don't make sense to me.

And heartfelt thanks to Connie Jones, Vice Chair, Gentle Teaching International (www.gentleteaching.com) and her husband Tim Jones, Executive Director of Saskatchewan Alternative Initiatives (www.saionline.ca) who provided invaluable feedback on a very important and sensitive aspect of this story: the special needs community. They are both deeply involved in supporting people with intellectual disabilities, educating those who work in this field, developing respectful, compassionate, individualized programming, and challenging and changing antiquated beliefs. Any missteps are mine alone. Thank you, Connie for sharing your wisdom. I am blessed to call you sister; to be able to call you friend is a gift from heaven.

Chapter One

NOTHING MARRED A triumphant homecoming like the secret, certain knowledge of failure. But if modeling in New York City had taught Deirdre Cash anything, it was how to put on a good face, no matter what fresh chaos was breaking out around her.

She stood on the porch at her parents' Montana ranch home, shivering—or rather, *hyperventilating*—in the frigid spring air while pretending to take an important call.

The screen door clanged open. "Is everything okay, DeeDee?" Mom, worried, as usual. Light, laughter, and warmth spilled out from behind the kitchen door. "Supper is waiting."

Joanie Cash-Henley was never happier than when feeding her family, and DeeDee's return had sent her into a cooking, cleaning, and caregiving frenzy.

DeeDee pasted on a smile and held her hand over the phone. "Everything's great, Mom. Be right there."

She loved her family with all her heart, but she'd rather they believe she was here because of crowd and camera fatigue instead of no callbacks and eviction. "I have to go, Jon," she said, even though there was no one on the line.

Jon wasn't speaking to her.

Her former agent, ex-lover, and worst mistake—though to be fair, there were a lot of contenders for that title—had dumped her three weeks ago, citing cosmetic surgery and a personality transplant as the only way to resurrect DeeDee's languishing career.

DeeDee had responded by suggesting Jon perform an anatomically impossible act—only to later realize she'd proved his last point.

Impulse—one. Control—zero.

No heartbreak on either side; they'd been beneficial to each other for a time, but now they weren't. So, what did a selfish, spoiled ex-model with few discernible skills and even fewer friends do when her bridge to the future lay in smoking ruins?

She went home. Where, as the saying went, they *had* to take you in.

"It's cold out, honey," her mom said. "I'll get you a sweater."

"It's okay. I'm coming in now."

Her mom took her arm, giving it a gentle tug as she led her inside. "You're so thin. You need a good meal."

"Occupational hazard. I'm fine."

DeeDee took her place at the table and pasted on her happy-daughter smile, hoping no one would notice anything amiss. Why would they? She'd used the same smile the last time she was home and everyone bought it, even though she'd been dying inside.

"Norman, isn't it wonderful to have all our girls home again?" She took Norm's hand and gave it a squeeze on top of the table. Mom never did distinguish between DeeDee, Maddie, and Norm's own daughter Cynthia.

"I can't thank you enough for coming home, DeeDee." Cynthia's eyes glistened as she raised her glass of water. Four months into her surprise pregnancy, DeeDee's stepsister waffled between glowing and green. "I don't know what I'd do if you hadn't stepped in to save the day."

Yes, unemployment had come at the perfect time. DeeDee could salvage Cynthia's event-planning business and her own pride, all at the same time. Score.

Not.

"Happy to be here," she said, glancing around the table. "And a fashion-show fundraiser—how could I resist?"

Truth. Just not the whole truth.

"Took you long enough." Maddie, DeeDee's twin, had nagged her to death about returning to Marietta. "I knew you'd come to your senses eventually."

"It's great to finally meet you, DeeDee." Mick, the man seated next to Maddie, gave her a teasing grin. "I've heard so much about you."

"I bet." DeeDee arched a look between the two of them. Mick's naturally scruffy-jawed appearance was the sort of thing stylists worked endlessly to recreate. She didn't wish misery on anyone, but Maddie already had a career and an apartment… not to mention the good personality. How was it fair that she got a great guy, too?

Between Maddie and Mick, and Cynthia and her fiancé Chad, there was enough romance in the room to put a girl off her food.

And to remind DeeDee that she was now the only unattached daughter.

The third wheel.

The seventh person at a table for six.

The last lone banana on the rack that no one picked.

Men stared at DeeDee all the time. But never, not once, had one looked at her the way the men at this table did their women.

"Everything smells great, Mom," DeeDee said, trying to shift the conversation.

She'd left Montana by choice and in the pursuit of better things. In the meantime, her family's lives had gone on without her. If she felt left out, left behind, well, what did she expect?

"I, for one, am ready to dig in," Norm said, holding out his hands to the person on either side of him. Everyone linked hands and bowed their heads while he said grace. Maddie caught DeeDee's eye across the table. Despite her mood, DeeDee had to stifle a giggle.

Some things, at least, never changed.

"Eat up, everyone." Mom pressed the bread basket into DeeDee's hand. "I made all your favorites, just the way you like. Lasagna with lots of cheese and spinach, garlic bread, and Caesar salad."

As if.

DeeDee passed the basket to Maddie. "Mom, I haven't eaten pasta or bread in months."

"I thought as much," she said. "You can't get good home cooking like this in New York City."

"Make sure to leave room for dessert." Norm looked pleased, like he was announcing a special surprise. "I bought a gallon of rocky road ice cream, to celebrate."

Her favorite.

"Ice cream," Cynthia murmured, putting down her fork. Her lips had gone white.

"Is she going to…?" DeeDee looked at Chad, feeling her own stomach turn over. She'd always been a sympathetic puker.

"I'm okay." Cynthia swallowed. Reaching a shaking hand for her water glass, she brought it to her mouth, took a tiny sip, and swallowed.

"Norman," her mom said, oblivious to the other end of the table, "I baked lemon-meringue pie and DeeDee's favorite chocolate cheesecake. You didn't have to get ice cream, too."

Cheesecake.

"All I've got is my face and my figure," DeeDee said, one

eye on Cynthia. "Fatten me up too much and I'll be living in your basement for the rest of my life."

"You've got more than that going for you." Cynthia burped delicately. "Oops. Excuse me."

"Speaking of chocolate." Maddie pushed her chair back and grabbed a package from the buffet. "I brought some of Sage's salted-caramel chocolates, too. She says hi and welcome back, DeeDee."

The famous Copper Mountain Chocolates. When would the torture end?

"Since when are you pals with Sage Carrigan?" she asked. Due to their popularity with the male population, the Cash twins had never been overburdened with female friends.

"Most people are pretty great when you take time to get to know them," Maddie said. "You'll see."

Maybe. Maybe not. DeeDee had never seen the point in investing in relationships she wouldn't be around long enough to enjoy.

"I've got frozen yogurt for you anyway, Norman," her mom added. "Last thing you need is pie."

"Like hell, woman." Norm sent a wink DeeDee's way. Maddie, Cynthia, and Mom started talking at once then, about Norm's diet and exercise, his cardiologist's recommendations, and how they each believed the other was pushing the man they all loved into an early grave.

DeeDee's throat tightened as she returned Norm's smile. Though he'd come late into their lives, the gentle man was the only father she and Maddie had ever known. She couldn't bear it that they'd nearly lost him, that she hadn't been here when it had happened, or that she'd clung to blissful ignorance rather than face the fact that she didn't have the gonads to deal with pain.

Panic bubbled up in her chest.

She grabbed for the salad bowl and helped herself to an enormous serving of greens, sans croutons.

The garlic bread, dripping with herbed butter, smelled amazing, and the edge pieces of lasagna had extra cheese, bubbled and crispy from the oven. She scraped the cheese off a small inside piece as she watched everyone else enjoy the feast.

How nice it must be to not worry about every calorie that passed your lips.

And then it was time for dessert. The final gauntlet.

"People keep asking what magazines you were in," her mom said as she handed around plates. "I looked and looked, but I never saw you in them."

It was the question DeeDee dreaded the most. "I wasn't doing that kind of modeling, Mom. It's a huge industry. There's a lot more than magazines."

"Tell us about your average day," Chad urged.

Now there was a face—and a personality—that New York would love. Chad could have a career doing orthodontia ads with that smile of his. He wasn't just being polite, either. He was a genuinely nice guy—for a cowboy.

"It's pretty boring to outsiders." DeeDee squirmed. There wasn't much she loved more than attention. So why did her back itch like she'd contracted poison oak? "Hair and makeup. Changing outfits a million times. Sitting around while you wait for the stage manager and the photographer to quit feuding, or for the light to cooperate. That sort of thing."

"That's why I knew you'd be the perfect one to help with the fundraiser." Cynthia's face was the color of seafoam. She shook her head at the plate that was offered to her.

"How's the cheesecake?" her mom asked.

DeeDee forked a small piece into her mouth. The crunchy cookie crush contrasted with the smooth cream cheese, which made the bittersweet dark chocolate layer even more intense. She groaned. "Even better than I remembered."

"To think we have a real, live celebrity in our family," Norm said to Cynthia. "Tell us more, DeeDee."

Cynthia shoved her chair back and ran from the table, fingers pressed to her mouth.

"Is she like this all the time?" DeeDee asked.

"Comes and goes." Chad got up to follow his fiancée. "But mostly, yeah. You see why she needs you. Carry on."

She'd rather not. The conversation, not to mention Cynthia's nausea, was making her stomach hurt. DeeDee toyed with her dessert, buying time.

She had plenty of stories to entertain them with. It had

been so much fun, at first. Eccentric designers, flamboyant photographers, bigger-than-life characters, narcissism galore, ambition and egos everywhere, everything bright, sparkly, and pretty.

But how quickly the glamour had faded. Those first few weeks of excitement turned first to routine, then to boredom, then to anxiety as she spent more and more time waiting around, listening to the other girls complain about their high-rent condos, hearing about parties she wasn't invited to, boyfriends they didn't appreciate, food they wanted but couldn't have, and drugs they weren't supposed to have but often did.

Suddenly, DeeDee needed to get out of there. She pushed back her chair abruptly.

"This has been wonderful, Mom, but I'm wiped." She needed to get some air, to not have any more questions thrown at her, or mine fields unknowingly tripped. Her stomach twisted again, another ulcer, probably.

"But you haven't finished your cheesecake." Disappointment creased her mom's forehead.

"I'll take it to go. Mick, Maddie, do you mind? Jet lag and all." DeeDee gave a great, huge yawn that wasn't entirely an act.

"Don't forget Sage's caramels." Mom pressed the package into DeeDee's hand. The copper ribbon was undone, releasing the rich, buttery caramel scent, underscored by cocoa. "Get some rest, honey. Love you. See you soon, right?"

"You bet, Mom. Love you, too. Thanks for everything."

"You leaving already?" Cynthia reappeared, Chad at her side.

"Yup, sorry, exhausted. I'll talk to you about the show tomorrow, okay, Cyn?"

While Maddie and Mick gathered their things, DeeDee escaped to the porch once more. She bent over slightly, her hands on her thighs, and sucked the cool evening air into her lungs. She'd forgotten how great fresh air tasted.

She'd forgotten how great a lot of things tasted.

It was better that way.

"You okay, DeeDee?" Mick asked as he walked to his pickup truck.

"Fabulous. Spectacular."

DeeDee had hitched a ride with Mick and Maddie, and now he drove them back to Maddie's apartment in town. DeeDee suspected she was cramping their style by bunking with her twin, but honestly, that was too bad for them. DeeDee would go mad if she had to stay in her old room at the ranch with their parents.

Besides, Maddie spent half her time at Mick's place, a rat-infested fishing lodge or something, out on the lake. It wasn't like he and Maddie would have to make out in the truck like teenagers.

"Here are the keys," Maddie said when they arrived at her apartment complex. "Go ahead. I'm going to say good-night to Mick."

They *were* going to make out in the truck like teenagers.

DeeDee grimaced. "I hope you've got wine."

Maddie tossed her the Copper Mountain Chocolates. "Better."

Chocolate she shouldn't eat. Stories she wouldn't tell. Regrets she couldn't escape.

"I DON'T WANNA have oatmeal."

Isaac Litton plopped a ladle-full into a bowl and set it in front of his brother. Their place still wasn't properly un-packed yet, and a pile of boxes sat on the table next to Mark's bowl. "Oatmeal is good for you."

Mark stuck out his plump lower lip and crossed his arms. He was twenty-four, but glared at Isaac with the stubborn-ness of a toddler.

"I don't have time to argue, Mark." The expensive com-panion their mother had hired for him three years ago had catered to the boy's sweet tooth, and Isaac was having a heck of a time breaking him of the habit.

"Can I have brown sugar?"

"You can have raisins."

"I want brown sugar and cimmanin."

The long tongue characteristically seen in people with Down syndrome gave Mark a speech impediment that was simultaneously endearing and annoying. Isaac hated it when things Mark couldn't help made him the object of ridicule. Mark himself never seemed to notice, which made it even worse to Isaac's way of thinking.

"Raisins are sweet enough. Here's your milk. You'll be late for work if you don't eat."

"Don' wanna go to work."

"Mark, we've been over this. You're still adjusting. You'll like it once you get used to it."

Mark didn't like the May Bell Care Home day program, but he had to do something while Isaac was working. The coordinator, Mrs. Hatcher, was a new addition since Isaac had first checked the place out several months ago. While she wasn't exactly warm and cuddly, she was organized and reliable, so Isaac had peace of mind knowing that for five hours, four days a week, Mark couldn't wander off or get hurt.

Isaac refused to put him in an institution. Except for a few periods of respite care in a group home, Mark had spent his life with their mother. Now, newly married to a decent guy who wanted to show her the world, she deserved some freedom, and Isaac was happy for her.

When Mom had hesitantly approached him, teary with new love and dreadful guilt over her special-needs son, Isaac immediately decided to adjust his lifestyle to accommodate Mark. He would strike out on his own. He'd reached the point in his career where he could manage his clients' investment portfolios from anywhere, and eighty-hour workweeks in a huge firm weren't doing him any favors.

Being able to work from home, while enjoying a quieter, slower life, had seemed like the perfect way to start getting to know his brother again. While driving through Montana on business several years ago, Isaac had stayed a few nights at a bed and breakfast in Marietta, and the little town had stuck in his mind. Real estate was reasonable, the people were friendly, and the air was fresh and clean.

Maybe he'd take up horseback riding again. Start some hobbies with Mark. Get involved in the community.

It had sounded so simple, so romantic. So doable.

Three weeks after the move, Isaac was still reeling from the hard landing of reality.

"Why can't I stay home with you, Isaac?" Mark pushed a spoon through his oatmeal. Routine was vital to his well-being. Unfortunately, they'd yet to establish one.

"We've been through this, Mark. I've got to work. And so do you. Your work is at the May Bell Care Home."

His phone buzzed and Isaac grabbed it off the counter, noting with dismay that the caller, a longtime investor looking to expand his holdings, was a half hour early.

"Isaac Litton," he said, pulling a paper towel off the roll and handing it to Mark.

"I want brown sugar," Mark said.

Isaac gestured at Mark to eat his breakfast. He'd planned the call for after his brother was safely on the bus, but some things couldn't be helped. He went downstairs to his office to take the call in relative quiet.

The client had just begun outlining the details of his inquiry when a thump sounded upstairs.

"Excuse me one moment," Isaac said, pressing the mute button. "Mark? Are you okay?"

No answer.

He took the stairs two at a time, to find his brother on the floor in front of the refrigerator, crying and holding his ankle.

"What happened, buddy? Are you okay?"

Mark only had a few minutes before the bus was due to arrive. A knock sounded downstairs at the door. Was it the bus driver already? Was everyone early today, or was Isaac just late?

"I'll be right there," he called down the stairs, hoping his voice carried to the screen door. A moment later, the landline in his office rang.

He closed his eyes and took a deep breath.

"I wanted brown sugar," Mark sobbed. "I wanted to get it all by myself, so you'd be proud."

The landline continued to ring. Combined with the beeping of his cell phone and Mark's snuffling wails, it made him want to yank his hair out.

This wasn't how it was supposed to be. Not at all.

Chapter Two

THEY'D MISSED THE bus. Of course.

Isaac maneuvered his luxury vehicle off the residential street and onto the main road. It was only a twenty-minute drive to the May Bell Care Home, but that wasn't what bothered Isaac the most. It was the precedent they were setting. If Mark couldn't adjust to this program, Isaac had to find something else for him to do.

And there wasn't anything else.

"I wish I could drive," Mark said.

"Here we are." Isaac pulled to a stop in front of the building, shuddering at the image of his brother behind the wheel. He popped the locks and waited for him to get out.

"Have a great day, buddy. See you later."

But Mark was no more enthused now than he'd been at home. He crossed his arms. "I don't like work."

Mark's eyebrows beetled together, his hair flopping over his forehead. He needed a haircut. And his glasses were smudged and crooked.

Isaac took them off Mark's face and cleaned them with a

corner of his shirt. "It'll be better soon."

"Can we get ice cream instead?" Mark looked at him hopefully.

Isaac sighed. "Sorry, buddy. How about I walk you in?"

Mark blew out a breath, sending bits of spittle onto the dashboard. "Okay."

To his surprise, Mark took his hand as they made their way down the sidewalk. His brother's fingers were damp. Was he really that nervous?

The May Bell Care Home was a residential facility for special-needs people who required full-time professional care. The day program they offered provided the ones who lived in the community a safe place to go during the day and supervised activities to occupy their time.

Isaac had toured it on one of his fact-finding missions to Marietta. He'd spoken at length to the director of care, who'd assured him it would provide the social and occupational enrichment Mark needed.

Apparently, he'd heard what he *wanted* to hear.

Forcing himself to view it through Mark's eyes, he winced.

The flat-roofed building was an obvious addition, tacked on some years ago without any attempt to make it blend in with the existing structures, as if no one expected it to last. It had a cinderblock foundation, two windows, and no curbside appeal.

"Here we go," Isaac said, opening the door.

Immediately, his heart sank. When he'd toured it earlier, he'd entered from the care home proper. Today, as he came in from the outside door, the scents of fresh spring air, budding plants, and fertile soil contrasted starkly with the room, which was musty with glue, old paper, and body odor.

A wooden table ran the length of the room, and folding chairs were set up at intervals, about a dozen in total. Blunt scissors, popsicle sticks, and various other materials were laid out in front of each chair.

A mock-up of what Isaac guessed was their project of the day stood propped in a mason jar in the center of the table.

It was a flag with the words *Buy Now* on it. This was the occupational enrichment?

Social enrichment looked even less likely.

About half the chairs were full, with three stations taken by people in wheelchairs. Two of them were elderly men with vacant eyes and drool on their chins. The third was a tiny woman with gnarled fingers who bent over her project as if it were the most important task in the world. The other occupants appeared to have varying degrees of physical or mental infirmity, some participating in the task, some rocking, some moaning, and one muttering under his breath.

A middle-aged woman with frizzy hair pulled back in a ponytail hurried up to meet them.

"Mr. Litton," she said, tipping her head at Isaac. She wore a gray bib apron with the May Bell Caregiver logo on it. Mrs. Hatcher, Isaac recalled. "I worried when Mark wasn't on the bus."

"Sorry we're late." Isaac peeled his hand from Mark's grip.

Mrs. Hatcher turned to Mark, slowing her speech and pitching her voice higher. "Hello, Mark. Let me take your things to the locker."

"I'm hungry," Mark said in a small voice.

Isaac opened his mouth, but Mrs. Hatcher beat him to it.

"You know the rules," she said, taking Mark's elbow. "Lunch is at noon."

Mark jerked his arm back.

"Now, Mark," Mrs. Hatcher said. "Let's not start with this already. It's too early for a time-out."

Time-out? Her syrupy voice almost made Isaac miss the threat that lay beneath. Wasn't behavioral modification antiquated thinking?

"Say goodbye to your brother," Mrs. Hatcher instructed.

Mark threw himself at Isaac, his customary bear hug tighter than usual.

"I'll see you in a few hours. Okay, buddy?" Isaac could feel Mark trembling.

Mark walked away with Mrs. Hatcher, his shoulders hunched, his head down. As he approached the table, he threw Isaac a look of such misery that his heart turned over in his chest.

"Wait," Isaac said.

The woman stopped, her eyes flickering between Mark and Isaac. "Take your seat, Mark, while I speak with your brother."

"He didn't eat much breakfast," Isaac said. "He'll probably be happier if you let him eat his apple while he works."

Mark hovered at the work station assigned to him, watching the interchange.

"Mark, take your seat." Mrs. Hatcher's voice was sterner this time.

She turned back to Isaac and gave him a small, tight smile. "Mr. Litton, he'll be fine. We go through this every morning with him. He's only acting out because you're here."

"Acting out?" Isaac repeated in disbelief. "He said he was hungry. And he's been coming for two weeks. Are you saying that he's always hungry and unhappy when he arrives?"

He thought of the oatmeal Mark hadn't eaten that morning. Was his attempt to improve his brother's diet and lifestyle causing problems here?

"I realize that this is still very new to you," Mrs. Hatcher said. "I understand you haven't lived with your brother long, either. We, on the other hand, have extensive training and experience with people like Mark. Trust me when I say that we know what's best for him."

The subtle disapproval attached to her words annoyed Isaac. The truth of her words only made it worse.

"Change upsets our patients," she continued. "Strict adherence to routine is what allows us to maintain control and keep the day running smoothly. Ultimately, that's what everyone wants. Mark." She pointed a finger without looking. "Sit down. Get to work."

Mark took his seat, lifted his safety scissors, and began cutting the plastic sheets into large triangles. His bowed head and slumped shoulders said more than Isaac wanted to know.

"I'm sure that's what *you* want, Mrs. Hatcher," he said. "That and the fee I'm paying to have my brother in this program. And Mark's only your patient if he's sick, so don't call him one."

What was he doing? He needed Mark to come here. He couldn't look after him on his own all day. He'd never get anything done.

"What would you prefer I call him, then?"

Isaac looked over at his brother. "You can call him Mark."

Mrs. Hatcher's gaze hardened. Her shoulders went up as her lips disappeared. "Mr. Litton, the needs of our... participants... are our number-one priority. Are you implying otherwise?"

The little woman with the gnarled hands was watching them avidly, as was a man about Mark's age who sat across the table.

"I'm not implying anything," Isaac said. "I'm saying it flat out. I see Mark not being allowed to eat when he's hungry and being told to do a task he doesn't want to do. Mark's needs are not your priority, so don't tell me they are. I'd like to speak to the director of care."

"Ha!" The man across from Mark slapped his hand on the table. "Ha-ha!"

Mrs. Hatcher's face turned to ice. "The director is away right now. I'll be sure to pass on your concerns. However, my patients are becoming agitated, so I think you should go."

She took his elbow, much the way she'd taken Mark's earlier, and nudged him toward the door.

Isaac stood his ground. "Not until Mark gets his snack."

Mrs. Hatcher spun on her heel, went to the locker, and retrieved Mark's backpack. Finally. But instead of handing Mark the apple inside, she set the bag on the table in front of him.

"Looks like you're going home early today, Mark."

Mark jerked his head up. "I am?"

She turned to Isaac, a look of challenge in her eyes. "You are. Whether you come back or not is up to your brother."

"Yay!" said Mark.

"Yay!" said his friend across the table. "I'm hungry too. I want burgers. And fries. With Mark."

It sounded like boogers and flies.

"You want to take Paulie with you, as well?" Mrs. Hatcher asked. "How about Abe? Or Scottie?"

"Yeah, Paulie!" Mark said.

Shuffles and murmurs indicated more comprehension than Isaac had guessed. He lifted both hands. "Whoa, everyone. No need to be hasty. I'm looking to open a dialogue here."

"A dialogue that will be continued later, with the director, Mr. Litton." Mrs. Hatcher pulled Mark out of his chair. "Have a good day."

Mark clutched at his sleeve as Mrs. Hatcher shepherded them out the door, closing and locking it behind them.

"Don't get too excited, pal. Let's go get some food while I think this through."

Mark's loopy grin warmed Isaac's heart but not quite enough to make up for the chill of dread creeping up at the thought of all the empty hours ahead of them.

What the heck was he going to do now?

DEEDEE AWOKE LATE the day after the dinner party, grateful again that Maddie had offered to let her crash at her apartment. Mom was a little too excited to have her prodigal daughter home again, and evading her questions without outright lying was exhausting.

Her mom didn't need to know how much time her famous model-daughter spent running back and forth between coffee outlets, getting yelled at because the coffee wasn't extra hot anymore. What did they expect when she was getting orders for eight people at once? Or the times she'd had to run back to exchange a cup because someone insisted it was caffeinated when they'd expressly requested decaf. As if you could taste caffeine.

Her cell phone dinged, and she fumbled to pick it up from among the magazines, tissues, pens, and hand-cream vials she'd tossed on the bedside table.

It was an email from one of her former roommates, reminding her that her portion of the rent was due. The woman seemed oblivious to the fact that DeeDee hadn't lived there for almost two months.

Maybe she hadn't noticed. Or maybe she was jealous because Jon had picked DeeDee and not one of them.

DeeDee's stomach quivered. Moving in with Jon had been a huge mistake. She tossed the device into her bag without responding, pulled on her favorite silk robe, and went to do what she did best—get coffee.

She walked through Maddie's apartment, fingering the throw on the couch, looking at the tasteful watercolors on the walls. It was a little domestic and ordinary for her liking, but Maddie had never shared DeeDee's driving need to be different, to break free.

A note was propped against the now-cold coffee pot, a key fob next to it.

Make yourself at home! If you want to use the car, the keys are on the hook. I got a ride with Mick. I'm taking the afternoon off so we can catch up properly. See you soon! Love, Maddie.

Oh, Maddie.

DeeDee swallowed against the lump in her throat. She was so lucky to have such a sweet, generous sister. Some days, it amazed her they were related at all, let alone twins. Maddie seemed to have gotten all the goodness, leaving DeeDee a beautiful, empty, self-centered shell.

Me-Me-DeeDee. Ditzy DeeDee. It was what they'd called her in high school and for good reason.

After sniffing the coffee, she dumped it into the sink and started a fresh pot. She went to the living room and plopped into a comfy-looking overstuffed armchair to wait. Clementine, Maddie's little fur ball of a dog, leaped into her lap.

"Ouch!" DeeDee made shooing motions with her fingertips as the dog's nails bit into her legs. She'd have scratch marks on her skin.

Scratches. Scars. What did it matter now?

Clementine planted her hind end on DeeDee's thighs and stared up as if sending an urgent mind message.

"I don't speak dog, in case you're wondering."

The dog blinked. Licked her chops. Was she hungry? For a chunk of DeeDee?

"Get in line." She hesitated, then stroked the dog's silky head with one finger. Clementine's stubby tail wiggled and her pink tongue darted out to lick DeeDee's wrist.

"If that's a taste test," she said, "let me stop you right now."

The dog resumed staring. DeeDee stared back. She

hadn't been surrounded by so much quiet in a long, long time. What did she do now?

This wasn't an in-the-moment, waiting-for-coffee question, but a bigger, more global what-do-I-do-with-my-life-now question.

Part-time work for Cynthia wouldn't pay enough to cover her credit card debts, and she wasn't about to approach Maya's Models, the tiny local agency she'd dismissed in favor of New York. If it was even still operational, which she doubted.

The refrigerator clicked on in the kitchen, the sound like a gunshot in the silence. DeeDee jumped, and the dog let out a snarly yelp, scrambling off her lap to sit, trembling in outrage, at the door.

"Nothing personal, Clem," she said, her heart thudding in her chest.

If a woman screamed in an empty room and no one heard it, had it really happened?

Clementine whined, dancing back and forth in front of the door. A moment later, Maddie's key turned in the lock.

"Hello, darling!" Maddie bent to pick up her pet and nuzzled her.

"Hello, sweetheart," DeeDee returned.

"Did you take good care of DeeDee, my love?" Maddie asked Clementine in a baby voice. She waved Clem's little paws, then kissed her nose again. "Mick says hi. What do you want to do today? I'm guessing you haven't been out."

Her hair was mussed, her cheeks pink.

"Gotta watch the beard burn, sis," DeeDee said. "It'll wreck your complexion."

Maddie wiggled her eyebrows. "Don't care. It's totally worth it."

"Gag."

"You're just jealous."

"Ha." That was DeeDee's line. It had *always* been her line. As long as she could remember, people had been jealous of her—her hair, her skin, her legs, her lips.

DeeDee rolled her eyes and flung one leg over the arm of the chair. "I'm in the midst of a minor career reassessment. Last thing I want or need is a man."

But the best part about having a twin was also the worst part, and Maddie wasn't about to let her off the hook.

"You're having a major existential crisis," Maddie corrected, "and you're lonely. What's really going on with you? Don't think I didn't notice how you sidestepped all the questions last night. Career reassessment, my butt."

She snorted as she hung her coat up, then went into the kitchen.

DeeDee wanted to talk to Maddie, she really did. But admitting defeat... even to her sister... rankled.

"A girl can't come home without getting the third degree? Maybe fame and fortune's not all it's cracked up to be."

"Looks like your coffee's ready. Want me to pour you a cup? Cream? Sugar? Sodium pentothal?"

DeeDee let her head fall back and stared up at the ceiling. She didn't know anyone still had stippled ceilings. "Any chance you've got vodka?"

"It's one o'clock in the afternoon. The only reason you're back in little old Marietta, Montana is that the shine's worn off the Big Apple. You wouldn't leave on your own. You got ejected."

"Did I order a big piece of your mind or did I order vodka?"

Cutlery clattered and clanged.

"I speak the truth in love, sweet womb mate." Maddie handed her the steaming cup. "Now, start talking. What's really going on with you? I'm not blind. Those bags under your eyes aren't Louis Vuitton, honey."

"Thanks a lot, sis." DeeDee took a sip, letting the hot liquid trickle down her throat, chasing a chill that had set up so deep inside she wasn't even aware of it until it started going away.

Maddie waited, then gave an exasperated huff. "You want me to beat it out of you? You've been a ghost since Christmas. Before Christmas. Not returning my calls. Voice mailbox full. One word answers from texts. Do you know how worried I've been?"

Guilt twisted inside DeeDee's belly and she massaged the spot just above her navel, automatically checking the smoothness of her waistline as well.

"I came back when Norm was sick."

Maddie sniffed. "You were here for a week."

"I stayed until he was out of danger. What was I supposed to do? Put my life on hold indefinitely?"

Tension zinged between them. Unlike most people, Maddie didn't back down from her.

"Like the rest of us, you mean? Mom needed you, Dee-Dee. I needed you."

With Cynthia focused on Norm, all Mom's emotional havoc would have fallen to Maddie. Having already lost one husband, their mom had been a basket case.

"I know." DeeDee looked away. "It was a chicken-shit move. Sorry."

The anxiety that rose in her at the memory of that week threatened to cut off her breath. She'd been terrified. The second she could, she'd raced back to New York where she could pretend all was well, everyone she loved was fine, and no one was suffering, hurting, struggling, or afraid. Pretending. Putting on a good face. That was DeeDee Cash's talent.

"No, I'm sorry." Maddie hung her head. "I guess that's been building up. I didn't mean to dump it on you like that, though."

"Fair's fair," DeeDee said.

Their eyes met, Maddie's shining with tears. DeeDee's welled up in response.

"That's enough of that, then." Maddie took a deep breath. "Let's get back to the true story of what you've been up to and what really brought you home."

DeeDee looked away. She owed Maddie the truth. At least a portion of it.

"I'm not exactly the supermodel I led people to believe," she admitted.

"I kind of figured that since we haven't seen you in anything. I asked Mom what kind of supermodel has zero face recognition, but she just ignored me."

"I'll tell you what kind." DeeDee glanced at her sister over the lip of her mug. "The kind whose face isn't the focus of attention. I'm not proud of what I did out there, Maddie."

Maddie's eyes widened. "Oh. God. Don't tell me—"

DeeDee stared at her for a moment, then gave a bark of laughter. "No! Good Lord, Maddie! No porn, no table dancing, no escort services. Nothing like that."

Her twin heaved a huge sigh. "I'd support you, whatever your choices, you know that. But I'm glad to hear it. So, what *were* you doing?"

DeeDee swallowed. "You know that big-box hardware store that's going national?"

"Tool Barn?" Maddie wrinkled her nose.

"I played a clerk in one of their print ads. My agent made me take acting classes, and that's what they got me."

DeeDee's big break had come in the form of an unrecognizable side-view image of her in an orange ball cap and apron, standing behind a cash register. The image was emblazoned on flyers inserted in newspapers, which would end up lining bird cages. It was a onetime, work-for-hire fee.

It had taken her six months to pay Jon back for the acting classes.

"Nothing wrong with that," Maddie said. "Why didn't you tell us?"

DeeDee shuddered. Maddie's determination to be supportive was almost as bad as Jon's laughter.

"I also got a cable TV gig for a vaccine campaign, playing someone suffering from shingles. Have you seen shingles? It's a big, red, blistery rash. They made me look like I had the acne breakout from hell all down one side of my neck and shoulder. Thank goodness they shot me in shadow."

And that wasn't all. She steeled herself to be honest with the one person who'd understand and keep it to herself.

"But you know what's most famous about me so far? And I use the word *famous* loosely," she added.

"What?"

"My feet." DeeDee put a hand to her face, unable to look her sister in the eye. "Maddie, my feet are the face of Dr. Dorne's Corn and Callus Palace."

She peeked through her fingers. Maddie stared, slack-jawed. Then she burst into laughter.

DeeDee stiffened. "You don't have to be quite so delighted."

"Oh, but I do!" Her twin could barely get the words out. "This calls for chocolate."

Maddie went to the kitchen, continuing to giggle as she

opened and closed cupboard doors. Clementine barked, running circles around her legs. Maddie lobbed a beautifully wrapped piece of Sage Carrigan O'Dell's Copper Mountain Chocolate.

"You know I can't eat that." DeeDee glowered at her sister.

"Eat it anyway." Maddie returned her gaze steadily from over the rim of her mug. "You could do with some sweetening."

DeeDee gave up and bit into the chocolate. The dark shell broke apart to reveal a smooth buttery center that melted on her tongue and made her forget all her problems for a moment.

"Oh, my God, Maddie. This stuff is amazing." If she wasn't a model anymore, did it matter if she gained a few pounds?

"I know, right?" Maddie grinned. "It's the cure for everything. So, you're Princess of the Callus Palace."

"I'm trusting you with this intel, Maddie." She swallowed. "I left to become rich and famous. Instead, I'm broke and pathetic. How do I come back from that?"

Chapter Three

"SEE THOSE LITTLE purple flowers?" Isaac gestured to a blanket of lavender and white blooms poking up beneath the trees in Bramble Park. One of the things he loved about Marietta was having walking trails a few steps from their front door. He'd had to drive several miles from his Chicago condo to find nature.

"Can I pick them?" Mark's face was wide open with pleasure.

Isaac felt that awful combination of happiness at his brother's easy joy and guilt that there'd been so little of it in the past few years. Isaac was going to change that.

After the scene with Mrs. Hatcher at the May Bell, they'd gone to the Main Street Diner for a big breakfast of bacon, eggs, and pancakes—everything Mark wanted but shouldn't have.

Isaac didn't know what else to do.

He'd contacted his clients and postponed his teleconferences until tomorrow, but tomorrow wouldn't be any better. How could he bring Mark back to that place after he'd pissed off the person in charge?

In hindsight, he didn't know how he hadn't realized the environment wasn't sufficiently stimulating for someone as high-functioning as Mark.

He handed his brother a disposable camera. "How about you take pictures instead of picking them? That way, other people can enjoy the flowers too."

On the other side of the park, two women ran their way. Even from a distance, Isaac could tell they were pretty. Marietta wasn't just friendly; it had an unusually high percentage of extraordinarily attractive residents.

Maybe it was his imagination.

Or maybe simply knowing that none of them were Jodi-Lyn allowed him to see pretty women again. Not that he was looking. Now that he was on the other side of the relationship, he recognized his lovely ex-fiancée symbolized everything that had been wrong with his old life. Wrong, selfish, shortsighted, and superficial.

That was the old Isaac.

He was still driven to succeed, but now he worked from home in jeans or sweatpants and went to the park with his kid brother, who may not be a kid anymore, but would always need him.

Mark immediately began snapping pictures, and Isaac suspected at least half the roll would be shots of his finger. Maybe an inexpensive digital camera would be a better option.

"Come on," he said. "We've got our workout gear on. Let's try some running. We need to work off those pancakes, right?"

He jogged in place, hoping to get some enthusiasm out of Mark. At the group home where he'd stayed before the move to Marietta, Mark had added ten pounds to his already-hefty frame. Isaac was determined that his brother would learn to enjoy a healthy, active lifestyle, nutritious food, and hopefully make some new friends.

Unfortunately, Mark's easygoing nature turned mulish when it came to giving up sweets, and the only way to get him to exercise was to trick him into it, something Isaac objected to on principle but was now rethinking.

"Running makes my feet hurt." Mark screwed up his face and danced from foot to foot as if he had to pee.

"Do you have to go to the washroom? I asked you twice before we left the diner."

"No. My feet hurt. I wanna take more pitchers."

"We'll run from this tree to that lamppost, then you can take more pictures. Okay, buddy?"

Mark twisted his lips, then gave a huge exhale. "Okay."

He groaned loudly with every step. Isaac bit back a smile and joined him. Every little bit of progress counted.

As they made their way across the park, he recognized one of the pretty women as the real estate agent who'd sold him his house.

"Is that Maddie?" Mark asked, perking up. Mark had his

own fondness for pretty women and had enjoyed Madeleine Cash's company immensely. He'd begged Isaac to buy another house, just so they could spend more time with Maddie.

"It looks like it."

Mark had admired Jodi-Lyn at first too.

Madeleine was with a woman who could only be her sister, according to the unmistakable family resemblance. Genetics had been kind to the Cash women. Though the sister was a little on the thin side, she had endless, amazing legs and a body to match. It was too early in the year for the tight shorts she was wearing, but Isaac wasn't complaining.

"Maddie's friend is so pretty. Who is she, Isaac?"

"Don't know, bud." He raised his hand, getting an answering wave from Maddie. "But I think we're going to find out."

DeeDee bent over, bracing her hands on her knees to catch her breath, wondering what made Maddie think jogging would lift her spirits. Perusing the want ads this afternoon had been both humbling and terrifying, as was writing her résumé.

"At least if I die," she gasped, "I won't have to worry about job interviews."

The sun was going down, and she was freezing. She had to do something to stay fit now that she was back in the land of home cooking, but she'd underestimated the difference between the great outdoors and a climate-controlled gym. March snow still clung to the hollows beneath the huge trees in Bramble Park, and the long shadows they cast would leave the ground frosty come morning.

Maddie pulled up behind her, then reached back and tugged her heel against her butt to stretch out the front of her leg. "Hey, see those guys? I know them. They're new in town. They just bought a house from me. Let's say hi."

DeeDee followed Maddie's gaze and spied two men heading their way, also in running gear. One was tall and athletic, the other short and wide, like a fireplug. Even from this distance, DeeDee could see he was handicapped in some way. The tall guy jogged backward and forward as if impatient to get going.

"No cowboys, Maddie." Never again.

"Isaac's not a cowboy." She grabbed DeeDee's elbow and lowered her voice. "He's in finance. Private investing or something. Money management, I think. I'm not sure. And I'm not talking about your love life. Last time I spoke to him, he was looking to hire someone."

"If you saw my bank statements, you'd realize that finance is not my wheelhouse."

"Never mind that. How would you feel about being a care aide?"

DeeDee laughed. "Care aide? This is me you're talking to. Those are not words commonly associated with me." She glanced at the two men again. "Especially if you're talking about short-bus, there."

Maddie shot her a disapproving look. "Really? You're better than that, DeeDee."

A pang of remorse tweaked her stomach. It was just a joke. "Don't bet on it."

"His name is Mark, and he has Down syndrome. He's Isaac's brother and a real sweetie."

"Then he doesn't deserve me. Mom replaced Goldie the Goldfish twelve times and I didn't even notice."

Maddie waved away her concerns. "You were eight. You've grown."

As they watched, the tall man bent over the short guy, patting his back or something. It was an awkwardly nurturing gesture, the wild-animal power of the man contained, tamped down, channeled into an unfamiliar outlet. It tweaked something inside her—that kindness.

"What makes you think he'd even consider hiring me?"

Maddie shrugged. "Gut instinct."

"What's his story?" DeeDee asked. "Another gorgeous cowboy who inherited a fortune from some long-forgotten relative?"

Marietta seemed to be overrepresented with men like that. Chad and Eric Anders, Austin Sweet, even Maddie's boyfriend Mick.

Technically, Maddie and DeeDee were heiresses themselves, though they'd blown through their trust funds years ago.

"He's not a cowboy. I told you. Here they come. Let me do the talking, okay?"

Maddie tended to believe she knew best about everyone, and she was right just enough to be annoying.

DeeDee couldn't afford to be fussy about work anymore, but she still preferred to make her own choices. Then, as the men came nearer, thoughts, worries, and concerns of all kind slipped away.

A shaft of sunlight burst through the mountains as the taller one came into clear view, painting him with the last of the gold and scarlet rays, first his head, then shoulders, then body and legs, like a hero emerging from the shadows in a movie. Time slowed and oh-em-gee.

Gorgeous was an understatement.

He had the easy, long-limbed walk of a man at ease with his power, comfortable with himself inside and out. And what an outside it was, olive-toned skin with a shadow of stubble on his jaw. Full lips tipped up in a slight smile, and wavy dark hair that fell across his forehead. He moved with the kind of masculine grace that made her think of wild animals. Leopards. Tigers.

No. Mustangs, all bunching, flexing muscles—speed, power, and danger.

If the Hallelujah chorus had started up, a flock of doves fluttered from the trees behind him, and a rainbow formed overhead, DeeDee would not have been surprised. It was only fitting.

But then the shorter man came out… and the needle on the record player of DeeDee's vinyl fantasy screeched to a stop.

"Hi, Maddie, hi! I took pitchers of flars." The round dude had a halting lisp and robust lungs. Thick glasses slid down his nose. He turned to DeeDee. "What's your name? I'm Mark. You're even prettier than Maddie. You cold? You wanna borrow my jacket?"

Before DeeDee knew what was happening, she was enveloped in the tent-like garment. She shivered, wrinkling her nose at the slightly sour smell, then tried to shrug it off. "I'm okay, thanks."

Children always made DeeDee nervous. Children in grown-up bodies were far, far worse. She didn't know how to behave around them. She never could tell what they were going to do or say. And they were so often sticky.

"DeeDee," Maddie said, her eyes glittering with excitement. "This is Isaac Litton and his brother Mark. Isaac and Mark, my twin sister, Deirdre Cash."

Isaac stuck out his hand. When DeeDee took it, she had that wonderful, awful feeling of all her senses going on high alert. Whether to press between the pages of a book, or recite to an investigator, the details surrounding this moment were important and must be remembered.

"Hello," she said, breathless again. "How are you?"

"Good to meet you, Deirdre," Isaac said. His voice was

deep, serious, but there was light dancing in the back of his dark eyes. His grip was warm and firm, sending tingles through her knees, all the way to her toes.

"Great! I'm… great." She was an idiot.

"DeeDee, DeeDee. That's a funny name." Mark grasped her hand and pumped it hard enough to make her hair flop around her face.

Isaac put his arm around Mark and tried to pull him away. "Mark. You're going to shake her arm off."

Mark's movements slowed as his face fell. Behind those thick lenses, his lashes flicked up and down.

"No, he's not." DeeDee pressed her other hand on top of his, noticing it wasn't sticky after all. "It's fine. Nice to meet you, too, Mark."

A big, loopy grin spread over his face like a sunrise. "You look like a peacock. So pretty."

Something about Mark's unvarnished admiration touched her deeply.

"Um… thank you." She searched for an appropriate response. "You also look very nice. Like… a nice… St. Bernard puppy."

Good job, DeeDee. Stop talking now.

"I like puppies," Mark went on. "What's a sane bunnerd? Your hair looks like toffee. I like toffee. Isaac doesn't let me have toffee. It's bad for my teeth."

It sounded like *teef*.

Maddie interrupted the flow of words. "Isaac, DeeDee's

just returned from New York and she's looking for work."

DeeDee turned to Maddie and opened her mouth, but got a discreet elbow in the ribs for it.

"She's not formally trained, but she's got tons of life experience," Maddie continued. "I think she and Mark would get along well together. It's always better when you have a personal reference, isn't it?"

"I don't know—" Isaac began.

"Gosh, look at the time," Maddie said, pulling out her cell phone. "How did it get away on us like that? We've got to go, but DeeDee can stop by tomorrow morning for a proper interview. I know your address, of course, so I'll give her directions. Good to see you both! Bye, Isaac. Bye, Mark."

She yanked DeeDee's arm and off they went.

"Bye-bye," Mark said from behind them.

"Seriously," DeeDee said as soon as they were out of earshot. "Have you always been this pushy?"

Maddie brushed away the question. "I have an instinct for things. This is going to work out just fine."

DeeDee rubbed her thumb over the opposite palm, which still tingled from Isaac's grip. "I hope you're right," she said.

Chapter Four

DEEDEE CHECKED THE address, looked up and down the empty street, and sucked in a deep breath. After getting used to the big-city bustle, quiet, postcard pretty Marietta, even on a sunny spring morning, gave her the jitters.

She yearned for the comforting, enveloping crowds, the busy streets, and the constant hum of activity that had become the backdrop of her life for the past year.

Here, she felt like a hamster plopped onto an empty dinner table. Anxiety was a reasonable response.

But what was the worst that could happen? She'd already met Isaac Litton, but she didn't know if she'd end up thanking her sister or blaming her for that. It could go either way.

"Big-girl panties," DeeDee reminded herself, wiping her hands on the inside of her favorite cashmere wrap. There was no need to be nervous. Anyone who could prance around on five-inch heels while people stared at her for ten hours a day, without producing a drop of flop sweat, could handle one little meeting.

Except this was no ordinary meeting. This was a job interview with a financial advisor-slash-Greek-god-slash-jungle cat-slash-protective-big-brother, and whatever Maddie said, it was a good bet he expected some skills besides party planning and putting on a bra one-handed.

No wonder DeeDee was spiraling into antiperspirant failure.

Nevertheless, she girded her loins and approached the wide porch steps fronting Isaac Litton's restored Victorian two-story.

She lifted her hand to knock, but the thunder of footsteps inside made her pause. A door slammed.

Voices argued. One loud, one softer.

She took a step back.

The heavy front door flew open and she jumped back even further as Isaac Litton appeared, taller and broader than yesterday—which was impossible.

"There's no time, Mark," he was saying. "Get your stuff and let's go. Oh."

Isaac skidded to a stop and froze, caught between the ornate wooden door and the outer screen door, blinking. A shock of black hair slipped over his forehead. The screen door slipped out of his hands and bumped his shoulder.

His wide, strong shoulder. That was attached to a broad chest, toned torso, and long, lean legs.

DeeDee had convinced herself that she'd exaggerated the

attributes of the man she'd met the previous day. Any reasonably fit guy could look good while out for a run, right? In real life, he probably wore bad suits and... a pocket-protector, maybe.

But the Isaac of today looked even better, unreasonably attractive in faded jeans and a red waffle-weaved T-shirt with long sleeves. If anything, his teeth were whiter, his hair sexier, his eyes darker.

And speaking of eyes. He pulled a pair of tortoiseshell glasses off and held them between two fingers at his side. Bad-boy professor.

"Whoa," she murmured. Too late, she clamped her lips shut. *Wherefore art thou, impulse control?* Same place it had always been.

A glimmer of a smile told her he'd heard, so she stuck out her hand, hoping to regain her dignity. "Deirdre Cash, in case you've forgotten. We didn't get much chance to talk yesterday."

His grip was just as warm and firm as she remembered, too. He hadn't shaved since then, and her fingers itched to test the stubble.

"Am I early? For the interview?" When he still didn't say anything, she added, "For the, um, position?"

She couldn't even bring herself to say the words *care aide*. Maybe he could use her as an office assistant, instead. She could imagine herself being at least somewhat useful in that arena.

"Right. No. It's fine." He glanced at his watch. "Time got away from us this morning. Listen, Ms. Cash, I don't think this is going to work out. Sorry to waste your time."

His quick dismissal irked her. She was tired of being rejected. "May I ask why?"

He glanced wordlessly over her wrap and raw silk pantsuit. "Let's just say it doesn't seem like a good fit."

DeeDee bridled. She wore the latest in professional attire from one of New York's leading designers. Maybe she was a little overdressed, but this was her second chance to make a first impression and even if he didn't hire her, she would make sure he didn't forget her.

She opened her mouth to argue when the thundering footsteps sounded again, and the moon-faced brother appeared.

"Isaac, I don't want tuna salad for lunch. I want pizza." Seeing DeeDee, he pulled up sharply and gaped. "DeeDee!"

She took a step back, then recovered. If she wanted this job, she had to do better than that. "Um. Hello. Hi. We meet again, Mark."

"Are you gonna be my new friend?" Mark didn't seem to notice her babbling, apparently fascinated by the pattern on her wrap.

DeeDee glanced at Isaac. "I'm not... that is—"

A horn sounded as a snub-nosed yellow van pulled up across the street. The driver rolled down the window and called out, "Running late, guys. Let's go."

Isaac blinked and shook his head as if to clear it of cobwebs. "Again, I apologize for the inconvenience, Ms. Cash. Get your bag, Mark. We're already on thin ice with Mrs. Hatcher."

She stepped out of the way and watched Isaac attempt to get his brother's attention. Mark, however, was transfixed. At least someone appreciated her outfit.

"Like a rainbow," he said. "So pretty."

"Mark's on his way," Isaac called to the driver, motioning for him to wait. "Mark, where's your backpack? You just had it. Never mind. I'll get it."

He disappeared back into the house, leaving her standing on the porch with Mark, who still fingered the delicate fabric of her wrap.

Awkward.

"So." She cleared her throat and attempted to tug the cloth out of his hand. "You're off to…"

School? Work? A play-date? If he was going somewhere, why did Isaac need to hire someone?

Mark sniffed the hem of her wrap, then rubbed it against his cheek. "Mrs. Hatcher said I can come back to work, but I don't wanna come back to work. I wanna stay here, with Isaac. But he has to work, and I can't work with him. He said so." Mark's face drooped, then lifted. "Your hair looks like toffee. I like toffee. Isaac doesn't let me have toffee. It's bad for my teeth."

DeeDee bit back a smile. "So you said yesterday."

The lenses of his glasses were so smeared DeeDee wondered how he could see through them. She hiked her bag higher on her shoulder and considered the house. Banging and clattering suggested Isaac wasn't having any luck finding Mark's backpack.

"Isaac makes me floss. See?" Mark grinned widely, showing off his molars.

"Um, very nice," DeeDee said.

"So soft." Mark touched her sleeve. "I like cookies. Do you like cookies?"

"Sure. Why not?" DeeDee could see the driver pointing at his watch. "Shouldn't you go catch your bus?"

Finally, Isaac bounded down the steps and pushed the pack into Mark's arms. "Found it. Have a good day, buddy. See you this afternoon."

"I don't wanna go to work." Mark's pout brightened. "Can DeeDee come to work with me?"

"What, now?" DeeDee cringed. She hadn't meant to sound horrified.

"Don't be ridiculous." Isaac's voice was tight. "Go. Now."

"Uh-uh." Mark ran back inside. He was surprisingly fast for his size.

A hissing screech sounded as the driver gave up and put the vehicle in gear.

"Wait!" Isaac ran toward the sidewalk, waving at the bus, which did not stop.

"Bye-bye," Mark called from upstairs. More thundering, then he returned, an extra-large candy bar in his hand.

"You want chocolate?"

"No, thanks." DeeDee lowered her voice. "I think you're in trouble."

"Uh-oh." Mark's smile faded.

Isaac stood on the sidewalk, his shoulders slumped. Then he straightened up and returned to the porch.

"Mark, would you get me a glass of water, please?"

"I can stay home?" Hope filled Mark's face. "DeeDee can stay with me?"

She started to laugh, then turned it into a cough. He was kind of sweet—in an unkempt, badly dressed way.

More importantly, he'd just handed her a lovely little bargaining chip.

"It was good meeting you, Isaac," she said, holding out her hand. "Sorry you missed your bus, Mark."

Mark's face sagged. "You're going?"

"I'm afraid so," she said. "Have a nice day."

"Don't go!" Mark threw his arms around her in a crushing hug.

"Oh!" DeeDee could hardly breathe.

"Mark, that's enough."

Mark, apparently recognizing something in his brother's voice, released her, ducked his head, and scuttled upstairs.

"On that unexpected note, have a nice day." DeeDee straightened her wrap and stepped off the porch.

Isaac ran a hand through his hair, making the dark glossy waves appear even thicker. "Ms. Cash, wait."

She dropped her hand and widened her eyes. "Yes? What is it?"

He looked her up and down again, even more critically than before. "Do you have a valid Montana driver's license?"

"Yes."

"Criminal record?"

Her jaw dropped. "No."

"Substance-abuse issues?"

"No." She crossed her arms. "Though it's none of your business."

"It is if you want to work for me."

This time, she let the laugh out. "I thought I was a bad fit." Smiling, she turned to leave. *One-Mississippi. Two-Mississippi. Three-Missi...*

A phone rang from inside the house, followed by the buzzing sound of some other device.

"Ms. Cash. Deirdre." Isaac closed his eyes as if gathering his patience. "I'll pay you a hundred dollars to keep my brother quiet upstairs while I take this call. We'll talk once I'm off the phone."

The phone continued to ring.

DeeDee put on her best poker face and said nothing.

He took a deep breath. "Please."

DeeDee shifted her hair away from her neck. "Make it five hundred and you've got yourself a deal."

ISAAC LITTON YAWNED wide enough to make his jaw pop, took off his glasses, and rubbed his face. His day had started at dawn, as usual, despite being up until midnight the night before. It was how he worked. It was how he'd always worked. The market fluctuated constantly; client queries came in at all times of day and night, weekends included. He didn't mind.

But he was in his mid-afternoon slump. The teleconference he'd nearly missed thanks to Mark not catching the bus hadn't gone as well as he'd hoped. He was off his game, as was evidenced by the rash impulse to ask Deirdre Cash to stay with Mark. He hadn't expected her to pounce on his offer.

He certainly hadn't expected her to up the ante.

Isaac couldn't decide if he distrusted her as an opportunistic mercenary or admired her quick, intuitive reaction.

Her offer to drive Mark to the May Bell for the afternoon portion of his program had floored him. How had she convinced Mark to go? Mrs. Hatcher was willing to let Mark come for a half day, so what else could Isaac do but agree?

Isaac checked the time. He'd gotten a solid chunk of work done. In another hour or so, Mark and Deirdre would be back.

If Deirdre Cash could drive Mark to his appointments and look after him while Isaac was busy, he might get caught up. He might actually start to settle into this new life. It was exactly what he'd been hoping for, so why was he uneasy?

Maybe it was the clothes she wore. Her extraordinary beauty and glamour were too much for a job like this. Why would someone like Deirdre offer to work with Mark? She had no experience, no training, and no particular affinity for the handicapped. Not as far as he could tell, anyway.

But despite all that, she seemed to click with Mark.

She clicked with Isaac, too, enough to unnerve him. It wasn't just physical attractiveness; Deirdre Cash had an in-your-face spark, a willingness to go to battle that he found intriguing. No shrinking violet, there. Strategy maybe, but no passive-aggressive manipulation or pretense.

Nothing like Jodi-Lyn.

He shook thoughts of his ex-fiancée away. He'd wasted too much time already.

Regardless of Isaac's reaction to Deirdre, it was Mark's immediate positive impression that had pushed the balance in her favor—for now, at any rate. He'd continue looking for someone competent, maternal. A no-nonsense grandmotherly person.

Deirdre Cash would have to do until then.

He refocused on his stock analytics. Before he knew it, he heard a car door slam, followed by footsteps on the porch. He glanced at the time again. They were early.

"Isaac, Isaac!" Mark ran through the door.

Isaac got to his feet, working out the stiffness that came from sitting for too long.

"Hey, buddy. Did you have a good time with your friends today?" As always, the sight of his brother made his heart simultaneously swell with pride and clutch with fear. The mind of a child, in the body of a man, with a heart so open and trusting, ready to love anyone, do anything, give *everything*, that he was the perfect target for exploitation and abuse, never recognizing when the laughter was at his expense.

Deirdre followed Mark, her caramel-colored hair bouncing over her shoulders and her boot heels clacking on the wooden porch. "See?" she said. "Alive and well. You're welcome."

She crossed her arms over her chest and tossed him a triumphant smile.

"Thank you." An answering smile tugged at his lips.

"Isaac, Isaac!" Mark tugged on his sleeve, his face wide with joy. "DeeDee took me to the park! Mrs. Hatchet was mean. DeeDee said there was no call for that, so we left."

"Mrs. *Hatchet*?" He frowned. "Don't you mean Mrs. Hatcher?"

Mark was looking too gleeful.

Deirdre shrugged. "Have you seen that face? Come on. You were thinking it too."

"But Mark wasn't," he shot back. "What is he talking about, Deirdre? Mark needs that program. You can't just walk out. It might not be great, but it's all he's got."

She lifted her eyes to the ceiling and sighed, flipping her

silky hair over her shoulder. "That place is right out of *One Flew Over the Cuckoo's Nest*. Hatchet-Face walks around like she's got a—"

"Stop." Isaac pointed to Mark. "Go upstairs and pour yourself a glass of milk."

"Can I have cookies?"

Isaac forced himself to breathe slowly. "Yes. One cookie."

"Can DeeDee have cookies with me?"

"Mark. Please." It took all his patience not to snap. "Let me talk to Ms. Cash."

Deirdre spoke up. "Listen to your brother, Mark."

She didn't use the fake voice that so many people did when interacting with Mark, the voice Isaac hated but sometimes caught himself using. The too-high, too-bright tones that indicated discomfort and a desire to be anywhere else, doing anything else. No, Deirdre spoke to Mark the same way she spoke to him. Like he was just another guy.

Mark grumbled, but left the room. The fact he'd obeyed Deirdre but not him did not help Isaac's mood.

He turned to Deirdre. "What the hell happened?"

"That woman, Mrs. *Hatcher*, is not much of a people person, if you ask me. I didn't like the way she was talking to Mark. When I called her on it, she suggested we leave. So, we went to the park, instead, and here we are now."

Deirdre wrapped long fingers around the straps of the ridiculously large purple bag over her shoulder and stared at him challengingly.

Isaac scratched his head. He couldn't argue. Deirdre reacted to Mrs. Hatchet the same way he himself had. *Hatcher*, damn it, now she had him doing it. "It wasn't your decision to make."

"I was defending your brother."

She lifted her eyebrows and bared her teeth in a predatory grin.

Whatever passed for hackles on humans stood up on the back of Isaac's neck. How dare she mess up the plan he'd so carefully established for Mark?

He got to his feet. "Ms. Cash, your opinion of the May Bell program notwithstanding, it meets Mark's needs for socialization and occupation."

"Really? Is that what Mark says?"

He forced his voice to stay calm. "I spent a lot of time and effort researching his options, Ms. Cash. You spent five minutes there and you know better than me?"

"He hates it."

"He doesn't hate it." He paused. "Maybe he doesn't love it, but we all have to do things we don't like sometimes. That's life.

He reached for his wallet, peeled off five bills, then added a sixth and handed them over. "Here's your cash, with extra for your time. Have a good day."

To his shock, she lifted her lip and turned away from his outstretched hand.

"I'm having a very good day, thanks, and I'm not done yet. Nice fish." She moved to the aquariums and trailed a slender, pink-tipped finger over the glass.

"No tapping the glass. What do you want, Ms. Cash? With those nails and clothes, I doubt you've ever washed your own dishes, much less scrubbed a toilet, did laundry, or spent time with someone like Mark. You want to know about this position? Looking after Mark isn't easy. It's messy, unglamorous, frustrating, and sometimes just plain hard. Is that what you want?"

Why was he even asking her? It shouldn't matter what she thought.

"You'll find I'm a very flexible person." Deirdre bent over the fish tank, the movement pulling the fabric of her pants so that he could see the outline of her thighs. A little thin for his taste but very shapely.

Isaac swallowed.

"For instance, I've never been tolerant of prejudice, but I'm willing to overlook the fact that you're judging me entirely on my appearance." Deirdre straightened up and drifted to the other tank. "And not in a good way."

Good thing she couldn't read his mind.

She made her way to the couch, dropped the purple satchel onto one end, and lowered herself onto the other. The boots she wore would have been worse than useless if the April sunshine hadn't melted most the snow already. Why would a woman of her height wear heels—on pink leather boots no less?

His email program pinged, announcing that another message had arrived, but he ignored it. "Ms. Cash," he said. "I have work to do."

He gestured to the door.

She smoothed her hands along the sides of those endless legs, then crossed her ankles to one side, like she was posing for a photograph. It looked like the smile had been carved into her face. The curve of lip and cheek was still there, but the softness and warmth had disappeared.

"At least take my information." She reached over to the body bag—what was the proper name for purses that size?—and rummaged around, finally pulling out a manila envelope. She half stood and handed it to him. The movement made the silky material beneath that poncho thing shift just enough that he caught a glimpse of sun-kissed cleavage.

Instantly, he averted his eyes, feeling his cheeks heat up. He took a step back, bumping his legs against his desk. Just then, his cell phone vibrated in the back pocket of his jeans. He jumped and nearly knocked over the mug of cold coffee sitting next to his reports.

He did need to hire someone. Ideally, he needed more than a care aide for Mark. He needed a housekeeper. A cook. A cleaner. His and Mark's living quarters on the second floor were still covered in boxes, the furniture shoved up against walls or unassembled. They'd used the kitchen only for pizza and cereal so far, having not yet located the cookware.

The upstairs door slammed, making him wince. He had better get Deirdre out before Mark came down and invited her to move in.

"I'm sorry for the misunderstanding, Ms. Cash." He gestured toward the door of his office once more. "Good luck with your job search. If you'll excuse me…"

She got to her feet and took a step toward him. He topped six-foot-two, which put her at about six-one with those heels. It was rare he could speak eye to blazing eye with a woman.

She didn't look away, either, but stood as if awaiting a better answer.

Her jaw shifted. The carved smile returned. The battle, if not conceded, was at least on hold.

Just then, Mark lumbered down the stairs and poked his head through the door.

"Isaac, Isaac," he said. "I made a snack for DeeDee. It's Ritz crackers and chocolate wafer cookies and I did it all by myself and I hardly spilled at all. Come on, DeeDee! Come see!"

Mark bounced up and down.

Deirdre sent a sweet smile to Isaac, then turned her attention to Mark. "Have you got any tea?"

Isaac pressed two fingers into the place between his eyebrows, where a headache was beginning.

Chapter Five

DEEDEE SURVEYED THE upper level of Isaac's house after Mark led her there. It looked like a FedEx truck had gotten friendly with a US Postal freighter and produced an unholy legion of spawn in the form of unmarked packages all over their kitchen.

"Love what you've done with the place," she said.

"It's our forever home." Mark beamed, oblivious to her sarcasm. "But we're not really home yet. Isaac says when the boxes are gone, then we'll be home."

"I see." She wiped a streak of dust off her pant leg.

"I like peanut butter. Do you like peanut butter?"

"To eat, to wear, or as a murder weapon?" Gingerly, she lifted a frighteningly large knife out of Mark's hand. Peanut butter was layered all over the wicked blade, the handle, the counter, his hands, one cheek, and his glasses. No blood to be seen, thankfully.

She didn't understand why she was trying so hard. Mark was clumsy and awkward in his cheap khakis and a hideous T-shirt that hadn't been white for a long time. Bright eyes

x

sparkled above cheeks heavy with a five-o'clock shadow and below the worst bowl cut outside of a cult.

But something about him was irresistible.

DeeDee was no idiot. She'd most likely destroyed her chances of getting hired when she pulled Mark out of his program. Quiet, stone-faced Isaac Litton disapproved of everything about her. It was like he didn't even see her. In fact, the only clue that Isaac was a living, breathing man was when her neckline gaped when she handed him her résumé. And he hadn't reacted in a good way. He'd acted as if he'd accidentally witnessed her coming from the ladies' room with her skirt tucked into her panty hose.

Embarrassed.

And that just made her mad.

"What say we clean up this mess?" She handed some paper towels to Mark, and they began tidying up.

She wasn't what Isaac was looking for. Well, Isaac Litton wasn't what *she* was looking for, either. She just wanted something that would pay off her credit card bills and keep her occupied when she wasn't working for Cynthia. She did not want to deal with a sternly rumpled big brother in faded jeans that rode his hips like a lover and made her want to yank the hem of his shirt from his waistband to see how warm his skin was.

"You're so pretty." Mark propped his face in his hands and gazed at her.

"You have peanut butter in your hair." She really did not

want a sticky teddy bear of a groupie who needed clean clothes, lessons in food safety, and possibly deworming.

"What's going on up here?" Isaac entered the kitchen. He'd left the tortoiseshell glasses in his office. Why were some men so sexy in glasses, while others just looked like dorks?

"Decontamination," she answered. "Might want to have the knife talk with your brother." She waved the sharp implement and tilted her head at Mark.

Isaac's face blanched. "Mark. You know you're only allowed to use the knives in the drawer."

Mark's face crumpled into a pout. "They're all dirty."

"I'm sensing a theme," DeeDee said, biting back a smirk. "I have two words for you, Isaac—hazard pay."

"I believe our business is concluded, Ms. Cash."

In the office below, a phone rang again. Isaac ran a hand through his hair, looking between his disaster of a kitchen and the stairway.

"Is it?" DeeDee said. "I'm not so sure. What do you think, Mark?"

"Yay!" Mark clapped his hands and wiggled his butt in the chair. "Let's have cookies!"

Isaac Litton might not want to hire her, but he had a very large Achilles heel in the form of his messy chatterbox of a brother and DeeDee wasn't above pressing the advantage.

"What kind of cookies have you got?" She batted her eyes at Isaac. "It would be rude for me to leave now. Your brother would be so disappointed."

Mark lumbered past her, knocking her Coach Legacy bag off the chair where she'd hung it. It slipped, hit the seat, and tipped, spilling its contents all over the floor.

"Mark!" Isaac put out his hand and caught his brother by the arm. "Watch where you're going."

"I sorry, DeeDee." Mark looked crushed.

"No big deal, Markie." She grinned at him. "Help me collect my stuff and we'll see to those cookies."

Mark flushed and sent a sloppy half-smile to his brother. "She called me Markie."

Score.

"Mark, please go watch TV. I'll help Ms. Cash, but then she has to go."

His imperious attitude was giving her hives. And not just her.

"Don' wanna go." Mark's eyebrows drew together.

"No need. I've got time." She patted Mark on the shoulder. "I was promised cookies, and cookies I shall have."

She could practically see flames radiating off Isaac.

Mark hunkered down onto his hands and knees. He began scooping up lipsticks, tissues, loose change, and old ticket stubs and shoved them into her bag. She winced as his clumsy hands strained the seams, but what the heck. Surely there was someone in town who did leather repairs should it come to that.

"Ms. Cash." Isaac's voice was low, but there was no mistaking the steel behind it. Finally, she'd gotten under his skin. "It's vitally important to my brother's psychological well-being that he stick to his routine. You seem a little… freeform… for our needs."

"Really? Ten minutes coloring outside the lines is going to send him into the nuthouse? Cut him some slack, *Isaac*." She emphasized his name, determined not to let him bully her with his Mr. Big Boss Man antics.

Isaac was pressing his lips together so tightly that the skin around them was white. Beneath his patrician cheekbones, a muscle ticked in his jaw. If only he didn't hold himself so tightly, the man could have made a hell of a cover model. All that Mr. Rochester glowering.

"There, DeeDee. I did it all." Mark got to his feet. There was a streak of lip liner, Blushing Bride, on his forehead.

DeeDee laughed. "How did you manage that? Come here. It totally clashes with the peanut butter." She swiped a tissue over his skin, and Mark giggled.

"This has gone far enough," Isaac said. He took his brother by the shoulder and turned him toward the door.

"Isaac," Mark protested.

"Say goodbye to Deirdre, Mark. Then go wash up."

"Bye, DeeDee." Mark gave her a quick, lackluster hug before slumping down the hallway.

DeeDee noted the rigidity of Isaac's shoulders beneath the fabric of his shirt. She ought to butt out, but she couldn't help herself.

"Be careful, Isaac," she said, deliberately using a light, friendly tone. "Your brother will think you don't like me."

"I don't *know* you." Isaac flushed and the muscle in his jaw flexed, hard. "And neither does Mark. He's unable to discriminate between genuine interest and those who consider him a joke or worse. It's up to me to be sure that his trust isn't abused. You've disrupted my brother's routine, made him miss work, upset him, and got his hopes up. If I needed reasons not to like you, those would do it. However, there's no need to get emotional. My brother has plenty of his own friends already. Good luck in your job search."

Throughout Isaac's rant, DeeDee watched him. She had flaws aplenty, but she could read people, and what she read in Isaac was uncertainty.

She gave a little laugh and propped one hand on her hip. "You, Isaac Litton, are a fascinating man. You clearly love your brother, which says a lot about your character. You're skilled and knowledgeable and have earned an excellent reputation in your field, which speaks to your values and work ethic. But despite all that, you've lied to me repeatedly. You're *not* sorry. You *do* need help. Your brother is lonely. He hates that glorified sweatshop. And you know it."

His silence told him she'd hit the mark.

She sighed. "Okay, okay, I'll see myself out. There's no way we'd be able to work together anyway, not with your personality issues. You don't like me; I get it."

"Liking or not liking a person has nothing to do with

who I hire, Ms. Cash. I hire based on merit alone."

"Bull." She snorted lightly. "Mark likes me. That's what has you tied up in knots."

Isaac looked away. She hiked her bag higher onto her shoulder and paused in the doorway. It was important to leave a strong, lasting impression.

"You should listen to your brother and hire me, Isaac," she said. "He has Down syndrome; he's not stupid."

DEEDEE HADN'T INTENDED to return to Isaac Litton's place. She didn't need the humiliation. Unfortunately, the envelope containing her résumé also inadvertently contained the last of her head shots and she wanted them back. Hopefully, in a few months, she'd get up the courage to look for another agent. She certainly couldn't afford to waste expensive photos.

She hoped Isaac hadn't bothered to look inside. Who sent head shots out when applying for a care-aide job?

She knocked on the door, unsure whether to go in guns drawn, or to pretend yesterday hadn't happened.

Isaac opened the door, his eyes widening in surprise. "Hello again," he said. "Did you forget something?"

There was a dimple in his chin she hadn't noticed yesterday. The tortoiseshell glasses were back, framing his dark eyes, the academic touch at odds with the faded jeans and torn T-shirt. Someone was definitely getting detention.

She met his gaze squarely, opting for guns over pretense. "We didn't discuss my hours."

His jaw dropped, but then his posture softened. He leaned against the doorframe and crossed his arms, smiling.

"That's true," he said. "Because I'm not hiring you."

DeeDee wanted to smack him right in that chiseled jaw. She crossed her arms in a way that ensured her boobs pressed gently against her scooped neckline. She'd worn Maddie's pink suede boots again, but she'd paired them with a tunic-length cashmere sweater and sleek narrow pants. The pants were also Maddie's but since she had several pairs exactly alike, DeeDee saw no reason not to borrow them.

She looked fantastic. Yet, she might have been invisible, for Isaac's response.

"I remember it differently." She tossed her head. "Fact is, I saved your bacon yesterday. What do you have against me, anyway?"

"You're not qualified." But he stepped back and allowed her into his office.

"How would you know?" she shot back. "We didn't even discuss my qualifications."

"I read your résumé. You don't have any."

Back to pretense, then. She lifted her chin. The envelope was on his desk, where she'd left it. Good. She'd just grab it and go. "I could say I accidentally gave you an old version, but you've already made up your mind about me. I could speak ten languages and have graduated cum laude from

Harvard Business School. I'm betting I could have a degree in health care and a personal recommendation from Mother Teresa herself and it wouldn't matter to you. For some reason, you don't like me. Despite me being an incredibly useful, helpful, and pleasant person to have around, you've decided that I am not the one for the job. So, if you don't mind, I'll take that off your hands and be on my way."

One corner of his mouth tipped up. "Do you?"

She was breathing hard. "Do I what?"

"Speak ten languages?"

She huffed. "I guess you'll never know. I'll find someone who appreciates me for the gem that I am."

"The photos were a special touch." Isaac sidled past her, reaching for the envelope.

She leaped forward, elbows up, trying to snatch it out of his hands. "I changed my mind. I don't want this job. I withdraw my application."

Unfortunately, she ended up slamming into him like a roller-derby enforcer.

He spun around, knocked off balance, and then, an endless split second later, they were both on the floor beside his enormous desk.

"Well…" she said, when she could breathe again. "This is awkward."

Isaac shifted out from under her, a shock of dark hair falling over his forehead. His back was strong and lean. He had runner's legs, long and muscular. She'd liked the way they'd felt beneath her own thighs.

She squeezed her eyes shut. "Any chance you have a convenient case of amnesia? Worked for my sister and her boyfriend."

Inwardly, DeeDee groaned. *Great.* She'd made it sound as if she wanted him as her boyfriend.

Isaac got to his feet and held out his hand to help her up. He wasn't smiling with his lips, but his eyes were suspiciously crinkled.

"I didn't mean—"

"I know. Are you okay?"

"Oh, I'm fantastic. Never better."

As long as she could remember, she and Maddie had been criticized for going off half-cocked. Throughout their elementary school years, teachers informed their mother that what she saw as fun-loving spontaneity was in fact irresponsibility and lack of respect for authority. High school hadn't changed things, but they'd done okay. Graduated, gone to college. So, they'd played a few pranks; no one had gotten hurt.

Their younger stepsister Cynthia might argue otherwise. But she'd been a shy wallflower who needed to be pulled out of her shell. And it had ended with her meeting Chad, so if anything, they'd done her a favor.

She swept her hands down the sides of her pants and adjusted her sweater. Her hair was all over the place, but what did it matter? He didn't give a hoot about how she looked.

She'd been an annoyance to him since the moment she'd stepped foot in his house.

"I'm really sorry about that. Please say goodbye to Mark for me when he comes home. He's kind of sweet. Good luck with whoever you end up hiring. I guarantee she won't be as fun as me."

She sidled past him, adjusting her bag, an elegant Kate Spade cross-body this time, and attempted to look dignified. Isaac didn't respond. Was he embarrassed? Deciding whether to press charges?

Or, wait. "I didn't hurt you, did I?" She looked him up and down, but if anything, he looked better than before with a bit of extra rumple on him.

A strange sound filled the room. It took her a second to realize that Isaac was chuckling. He had a lovely voice, deep and musical, like a river of rich chocolate rolling over a green meadow.

She clenched her jaw. How dare he laugh at her! How dare he act all silent and sullen and let her go on and on, feeling bad and guilty and embarrassed when, to him, the whole thing was hilarious.

She sucked in a huge breath. She'd tell him a thing or two.

But before she could, he stifled his laughter and put a placating hand out toward her. He cleared his throat and shook the photographs out of the envelope.

"Mother Teresa, you say?"

Chapter Six

DEIRDRE CASH HAD tackled him. And she had plenty of qualifications—for a model. That explained the clothes, the makeup, the hair.

It did not explain why she, with her head shots and no pertinent training or experience, wanted this job. It did not indicate where she hoped it would lead or how long she intended to remain in his employ.

Not long, he guessed. Those Bambi lashes and big hoop earrings weren't made for a rodeo town like Marietta. Then again, she had family here.

Isaac had never met anyone like her. Still, she had helped him out of a jam yesterday, despite her high-handedness with Mrs. Hatchet. *Hatcher!* Damn it, that nickname was going to stick.

His mother would like Deirdre, but whether she'd trust him with her Markie was another question.

"I'm willing to give you a try," he said to her. "One day a week."

"Full time," she countered. "And I want dental. I'm

overdue for a cleaning."

He bit back a smile. "Two days a week and I'll give you a Starbucks card."

"Like there's a Starbucks in Marietta." She tossed her head. "I want full time. And I'll throw in my services as a personal trainer."

"A trainer?" This time, he allowed his smile out. "You saying I'm out of shape?"

Deirdre lifted a carefully arched eyebrow. "I wasn't thinking about you, but for the right price, I'd consider it."

Heat sizzled from her ice-blue eyes. She was flirting with him!

"I hate to tell you," she added, "but your brother needs to shed a few pounds. I'll make sure he exercises every afternoon and eats more nutritious snacks. I don't cook much, but I can do omelets, smoothies, and stir-fries. I'm also the queen of bagged salads."

Isaac considered this. They had eaten far too much frozen pizza recently, but Mark was so picky and Isaac hated battling with him. Deirdre obviously held to a meager diet. If she could inspire Mark to eat vegetables and become more active, then it would be one huge worry off Isaac's mind.

He hoped he wasn't making a mistake. "Three days a week. Ditch the fancy clothes. Wear sensible shoes. Jeans. Stuff you don't mind getting messy."

Another hair toss. "I can get messy and still look good."

No doubt about that. Clothing had nothing to do with

her beauty. She was a natural. She'd look beautiful in sackcloth and ashes. Or nothing at all.

Great… now he was imagining her naked.

When she first walked through his door, he'd have bet money that she'd never even talked to someone like Mark. And now she was lobbying to spend most her week with him? She had to be desperate and that raised bigger questions.

"Why do you want this job, Ms. Cash? You have no experience in working with intellectually challenged individuals. You're clearly not the domestic type."

She swallowed and pursed her lips. "I need a job, okay? There aren't a lot of options out there for someone with… Mother Teresa's recommendation."

His bark of laughter surprised them both. "Don't forget the Harvard business degree."

Deirdre's face softened. The brittle mask of battle gave way to a softer, slightly vulnerable expression.

"You're right," she said. "This isn't a job I ever saw myself doing. But your sticky, stubborn brother is also unexpectedly charming. This might surprise you, but not everyone recognizes my exceptional qualities as quickly as Mark did. That's tough to resist."

Isaac's throat tightened. Of all the things she might have noticed, she'd landed on Mark's character. How could he refute that? Mark adored her, and she seemed to enjoy his company in return. Hell, she was advocating for him already.

It wasn't smart, but it was admirable.

"A two-week probationary period, then a minimum commitment of three months."

She lifted her eyebrows. "That's dangerous for both sides. This works as long as it works. When it doesn't, it's over. No harm, no foul."

Exhaustion overtook him. He couldn't bear the thought of looking for someone else. He needed the decision made, the person hired, the work done. He named a wage slightly above the going rate, and she nodded.

"Fine," he said. "And if you can break his cookie habit, I'll give you a bonus. Deal?"

"Deal." She smiled, her teeth bright and perfect.

He took her hand and they shook, their eyes locked on each other.

A beneficial relationship for them both? Or mutually assured destruction?

DEIRDRE DIDN'T WASTE any time.

The next afternoon, Isaac sat down next to his brother, who, to his surprise, ate most of a cucumber, a slice of cheese, and even one of the high-fiber bars she'd purchased, commenting favorably about it, which shocked Isaac completely. Perhaps she really would be able to help Mark lose weight and get healthier.

She stood up, pulled her oversized bag, a green one today, onto the table and removed a shiny copper package from inside.

"Mark, you like chocolate, don't you?"

Mark nodded. "But my doctor said I'm not 'llowed because I'm too fat."

Isaac bit down the white-hot burst that always pierced his heart when he learned of another hurt inflicted on his sweet brother. People with Down syndrome were often overweight, but the way Mark spoke told him he'd heard it in a purely pejorative way.

"That's mean and stupid," Deirdre said. "Fat-shaming doesn't work. You need a plan, that's all. What if I told you that you could have chocolate every day and still lose enough weight to satisfy Dr. Dumbass?"

Mark giggled "Dr. Dumbass."

Isaac groaned. "Deirdre, please. His doctor in Chicago wasn't very patient, but Mark's got a new one here. I'd like to start off on the right foot. What my brother needs is more exercise, not more sweets. Unfortunately, I don't have time to take him running with me every day."

"He's not a Labrador, Isaac." She sounded disgusted.

"I'm not a Lad-ra-bor, Isaac," Mark repeated, highly amused.

"Maybe Mark doesn't like running, Isaac. Maybe he'd prefer walking."

"Running makes my feet hurt," Mark said.

"Or square dancing or pulling weeds or riding horses."

Mark looked confused. This was going downhill fast.

"I have a file to complete, Deirdre. Was there a point to all this?"

"Yes," she said. "Chocolate. But Mark, you have to earn it, and I don't mean the kind of chocolate you get at the gas station. I mean the good stuff."

"Isn't all chocolate good?" Mark looked confused.

Isaac looked at Deirdre. "He's got a point."

She shrugged. "Maybe. But it's better to have a small amount of something exceptional than lots and lots of cheap, ordinary stuff."

She'd obviously never been responsible for feeding a young man. Not to mention that she had the appetite of a chipmunk. He had yet to see her eat more than a few bites at a time, and it was always fresh fruit, salad, or yogurt.

Deirdre opened the package slowly, as if deliberately drawing out the suspense. "I brought some very special chocolate for a treat. This isn't factory-made crap. This is from a shop here in town called Copper Mountain Chocolates. The owner does everything herself, using single-source cocoa beans, all by hand."

Mark's face split into a grin. "I wanna make chocolate by hand, too!"

Even though he probably had no idea what Deirdre was talking about, Mark loved that idea, Isaac could tell.

Deirdre held up a small morsel between two fingers. Her fingernails were painted a delicate shell pink with white tips.

They weren't talons but medium length and nicely shaped. Just long enough to scratch a man's back without leaving permanent damage. He squirmed against the chair back, wishing he hadn't thought of that.

"This isn't the kind chocolate you wolf down without tasting. This is a treat to savor."

"Save her from what?" Mark said.

"Watch me. First, we smell it." She closed her eyes and held the candy under her nose. "Oh, man. This is good stuff. You try it, Isaac."

She bent toward him and a lock of hair slipped over her shoulder, tickling his hand. He reached out to tuck it back behind her ear, and she froze.

"Um, here," she said, shoving the candy at him. "What do you smell?"

He'd unnerved her with his touch. The idea pleased him, made him want to do it again. She played herself as such a together person, no weaknesses, no needs. Of course, it was a charade—no one was truly an island—but he wanted to find out more of what made her tick.

He sniffed deeply, holding her gaze. "Chocolate."

"Oh, come on." She huffed. "You're not even trying."

She lifted the candy to her nose and inhaled. Her nostrils flared gently, and he noticed a slight bump on one side of her bridge. The tiny flaw in her otherwise perfect features had the effect of making the whole picture more beautiful for the contrast.

"Try again."

He sniffed dutifully, but he was too aware of her skin, the line of her collarbones, that waterfall of hair that kept slipping over her shoulder.

"Sugar?" he tried.

"Okay, not bad." She held the candy up to Mark's face. "Your turn."

Mark sucked in through his nose, snuffling like a bloodhound. "Smells good. Like Easter."

"Like what about Easter, Mark?"

He frowned. "Bunnies. Bunnies and eggs."

"Good job, Mark. Easter bunnies and eggs are made of chocolate."

"I like chocolate bunnies." Mark gave a heavy sigh. "Isaac says I don't need chocolate bunnies anymore."

Deirdre threw him a disapproving glance. Isaac crossed his arms. He'd been hoping to distract Mark from the season's indulgence, and this wasn't helping.

"No one *needs* chocolate bunnies," she said, surprising him. "But it wouldn't be Easter without some treats. Small amounts of the very best, that's what you want. Listen and learn, gents." She inhaled again, soft and slow, then held the candy out to them for a second try.

"There's cocoa, of course." Her voice was low and melodic. "The richness of cocoa butter. Some people say you can't smell fat or sugar, but that's not true. You just have to try."

Mark giggled. She opened her eyes to glare at him, and he quieted instantly.

"There's a touch of bitterness, too, like coffee, but sweeter. Nuttiness, maybe. There's a push-pull going on that's complex and irresistible. Can you smell it now?"

Push-pull. Complex and irresistible. "Sure," Isaac said, but he wasn't talking about the chocolate.

"What?" Mark said, sounding confused.

"Never mind. It's time to give it a taste." DeeDee held up one finger. "I'm going to cut this one into quarters, and you're going to taste it one small piece at a time."

"I want a whole one." Mark's complaint had an edge to it. An unstoppable force was about to meet an immoveable object.

DeeDee put the piece on a plastic cutting board and pushed a paring knife through it one way, then across. "I've seen you eat, my friend. There will be no shoving or slurping or jamming it into your mouth to see how fast you can get it in. This is about extending the pleasure."

The way she said it had Isaac thinking of something entirely different from chocolate.

"Eating slowly," she continued, "helps you get the full enjoyment from something new and wonderful."

There was a sensuality about her that was completely out of place in his kitchen, especially with his younger brother hanging on her every word. It occurred to Isaac that he might invite DeeDee to lunch one of these days when Mark was at his day program. Talk with her about something other than business or Mark.

"I don't wanna eat slow." Mark's bottom lip stuck out. Thunder darkened his features.

"Then you don't get any."

Mark froze, then sucked in a huge breath and leaped to his feet, a raw, sobbing roar tearing from his throat. His thighs caught the edge of the table, tipping it, sending everything on it flying. His chair bounced backward against the wall.

DeeDee had unwittingly given Mark the worst possible response.

Isaac rushed to his brother, hoping to forestall disaster. "It's okay. Here, Mark. You can have the chocolate."

But Mark had already slid to the floor and was banging the back of his head against the wall, his face a mask of despair, unable to hear Isaac, oblivious to the proffered treat. Isaac's heart broke anew.

Forget lunch with DeeDee. Forget anything with Dee-Dee. She wouldn't want anything to do with either of them anymore. Isaac couldn't blame her. She wasn't prepared. She didn't have the tools.

Hell, he didn't have the tools.

"What did I do?" DeeDee stood as if at gunpoint, her back against the counter, her eyes wide, her color high.

Isaac sat down on the floor next to his brother and put his arm over Mark's shoulder, getting between his head and the wall.

"This isn't just a tantrum, is it?" she said softly.

Isaac shook his head. "It's okay, buddy. I'm sorry. Can we start over?"

"I don't understand." DeeDee shook her head, a look of devastation on her face.

Speaking quickly and quietly over Mark's sobs, Isaac told her about his brother's dismal experience in the group home. "He learned that whatever he loved most would be withheld, used against him in order to gain his compliance. TV. Outings. Food. Often with those exact words—*then you don't get any.*" Rage still bubbled at the memory. "I should have warned you."

DeeDee crouched in front of Mark, then hunkered down onto the floor, so that they had Mark sandwiched between them. "I'm sorry, Marco. I didn't mean to make you feel bad."

Mark sniffled. "Sorry, sorry, sorry."

To Isaac's relief, Mark's composure returned quicker than he expected. Maybe DeeDee had more tools than he'd given her credit for.

After a while, DeeDee asked, "Do you still want to try the chocolate?"

"One piece?" Mark said.

"That's the deal." She got to her feet and held out her hand to help him up. "This is the good stuff. We eat it a little at a time. Okay?"

"Yes." Mark opened his mouth wide.

She dropped the candy inside, and he promptly bit down, chewed, and swallowed, his earlier upset forgotten.

"So good. Isaac?"

"Isaac, now you." She turned to him, and his chest tightened. He opened his mouth. As she put the piece of candy onto his tongue, her finger grazed his lip. Electric heat ran from that tiny point of contact throughout his body, adding to the increasingly uncomfortable tension in his groin.

Closing his mouth, he let the chocolate melt. He could take instructions.

"So?" She watched him. Just for a moment, hunger gleamed in her eyes. It was there and gone so quickly that he might have imagined it.

"Aren't you going to have a piece?" Isaac asked.

Deirdre gave a little laugh, sweeping a lock of hair off her cheek. "I've had lots already. This is about you guys, not me. Tell me what you tasted."

He wasn't imagining the hunger behind those laughing eyes. What other pleasures did she deny herself? Suddenly, he felt challenged to break her.

"It's everything you said it was and more." He knew that if he was to tempt her, it would be with words. He wasn't skilled at wordplay, but that didn't mean he wouldn't try. "Smooth and silky on the tongue. Rich and dark. Complicated. Intriguing."

He spoke slowly and noticed she was watching his

mouth, as if she'd never seen one before. Her eyes were soft, dreamy, distant. Her hand fluttered to the bridge of her nose, then to her chin, and with a quick shiver, a swallow, and a nod, she seemed to come back to herself.

"Not bad. You'll never write food reviews, but that's a pretty good assessment."

Her voice was hoarse. A frisson of triumph ran through him. He'd gotten to her.

"Come on. Have a piece. Aren't you intrigued by rich, dark, complicated flavors? Or are you afraid that you won't be able to stop at one taste?"

She lifted her eyebrows. "Are we still talking about chocolate?"

Mark gave an impatient huff. "DeeDee, you're being silly. I want another piece."

She broke eye contact and brought her attention back to Mark, choosing her words carefully. "One piece a day, after we walk together for half an hour. That's the length of one episode of *The Big Bang Theory*."

Mark's favorite show.

"A whole episode of walking!" Mark gave DeeDee an incredulous look. "I can't do that."

Isaac held his breath. Was DeeDee's stubbornness going to send Mark into another meltdown?

"Sure, you can." She patted him on the shoulder. "I'll go with you. And when we're done, we'll each have a piece of chocolate. The good stuff. Every day. What do you think?

Deal?"

"Every single day?" Mark's eyes narrowed.

"You got it, buddy."

The excitement in Mark's voice for Deirdre's small affection stirred the guilt that slumbered in Isaac's belly. Isaac could have put more effort into figuring out his brother. He could set aside more time to be with Mark.

"And you'll go with me, DeeDee?"

A nip of envy joined the gnaw of guilt.

"I told you I would," Deirdre said, "so I will."

"Every day? Even when you're too busy?"

"Deirdre isn't here on weekends, buddy." Mark's caution saddened Isaac. "But I'll go with you then."

He could do that. He could rebuild Mark's trust in him.

"You will?" Wonder and longing, disbelief and hope, infused Mark's voice. He was so used to being relegated to the sidelines. Deirdre was changing that, and Isaac was grateful.

"Absolutely."

"And you and DeeDee will have chocolate with me, too?"

Mark sounded as if it was a thought too good to be true. More guilt twisted inside Isaac.

"Of course, I will."

"And you, DeeDee?"

"I bought it for you, Marco." She was suddenly occupied with searching through her bag for something.

"But you have to have some too, don't you? One piece a day? After exercise?"

Deirdre opened her mouth as if to argue again, but at the expression on Mark's face, she stopped. She looked down, then inhaled and touched the young man's arm.

"Of course I'll have chocolate with you."

DEEDEE HAD EATEN more chocolate in the past few days than she had in the whole previous year. She smoothed her sweater over the waistband of her jodhpur-style leggings, testing for any sign of weight gain.

One piece a day wouldn't pack on the pounds, would it? She could do that. For Mark.

And for Isaac too.

Turns out, the strong, silent type could flirt. Not very well, of course; no one could compete with DeeDee when it came to flirting. But she was delighted at Isaac's attempts.

She didn't want to think about why.

"Mark," she said, "why don't you go into the other room and watch TV for a while? I need to talk to Isaac."

He'd displayed admirable control after chomping down that first bite, making a show of letting the truffles melt in his mouth. But he was getting fidgety now. It looked as if his good nature had had enough.

"Okay," Mark said.

The second the boy was gone, Isaac turned to her.

"That," he said, "was amazing. You have a way with him. Are you sure this isn't the sort of work you'd like to do?"

Shock robbed her of speech but just for a moment.

"What are you saying, Ike?" She took a step closer to him. "Could it be that I've exceeded your expectations? That the incompetent, ill-suited applicant has turned into a paragon of virtue and skill?"

His eyes darkened, and he crooked one eyebrow. "Virtue? Really?"

"Skill, then."

"We never did talk about that résumé of yours. What other skills do you have that you didn't list?"

He touched her arm, running one finger up to her shoulder, then down again to her elbow. She shivered, but couldn't make herself pull away.

"You mean, besides the multiple doctoral degrees, commendations, and of course, the sainthood?"

"Yes, besides that."

Suddenly, his joking touched a nerve. He was fully aware that she had no other skills. She was an out-of-work model and an even less-successful actor. She had exceptional bone structure, she knew how to dress, and she thought fast on her feet.

"I have an excellent sense of the ridiculous."

"Ah," Isaac said. "That explains the handbags."

"Each one chosen to perfectly complement my outfits. They catch the eye, you must admit."

"They do that."

The way he was looking at her made something in her chest grow hot and tight, like she was standing under a klieg light in a sheer dress and granny panties. She had no need for his sympathy, had no intention of fishing for compliments, and only wanted only to turn the conversation back onto more comfortable ground.

She shrugged. "Mark likes me; that's why it works between us."

Isaac looked at her for a moment, as if trying to decide whether to argue with her.

"That's the remarkable thing," he said. "You've formed a relationship with him. I've seen him interact with a lot of people who look at him like a problem, a project, a task to be managed, handled. You treat him like…"

"A St. Bernard puppy?"

This conversation was veering dangerously off course. She didn't know how to handle compliments that didn't involve her looks.

Isaac laughed. "He's kind of like a puppy, isn't he? Affectionate, clumsy, always looking for approval. But no. You treat him like a person. You see him."

DeeDee understood what it was like to be invisible. The body who wore the clothes, the skin that showcased the product, a collection of features and limbs and movement.

"I see him as a messy person. There's a map of Texas in ketchup on that sweatshirt. He could use new clothes, Isaac."

"Are you volunteering to take him?" A shudder ran over Isaac's shoulders. "Because let me tell you, that'll show you a different side of him."

"I'm an excellent shopper."

"I suppose you would be." He looked perplexed. "You have a natural gift with Mark, Deirdre. I'm lucky to have found you."

"It's not rocket science. I'm just being nice to him." Nervous laughter bubbled up. Such a simple thing. If only she'd learned it years ago. "I'm lucky that most people are basically superficial."

"You're more than what you look like, Deirdre. It's what a person does that matters. And I appreciate what you're doing. With Mark, I mean."

Chapter Seven

"IS IT STILL morning sickness if it's three in the afternoon?"

DeeDee looked around the Copper Mountain Chocolate Shop, wondering what it would do for Sage's business if her sister ralphed on the floor. She and Cynthia were seated at one of the small tables off to the side of the shop, but they were still within view of the steady stream of customers coming and going.

After the successful taste testing of Sage's products with Mark yesterday, DeeDee wanted to keep a supply on hand, so she'd arranged to meet Cynthia here, where she could kill two birds with one stone.

She wished she'd gone out to Anders Run instead, where her stepsister could be as green as she liked in the privacy of her own home.

Cynthia held up a finger and breathed through her mouth as what looked like another wave of nausea passed over her. Then color flushed into her pale cheeks and a sheen of perspiration broke out on her forehead.

"They say it's a sign of a healthy pregnancy." Cynthia blotted her skin with a paper napkin. "Now, where were we?" Her cheekbones stood out prominently, sharply visible through her almost-translucent complexion. Heroin-chic, very eighties. Not a good look for Cyn.

"Are you sure you can concentrate? Maybe you should go home and lie down. With a bucket."

"I'm fine." Her voice softened. "But once more, I'm so grateful for your help, DeeDee. I know it's not what you planned... coming back here like this..."

Her gaze was warm with sympathy, and DeeDee shifted in her seat. Embarrassment flooded her cheeks with heat. "Maddie told you."

"Don't be mad. We've all been worried. Besides, I had a feeling things weren't quite as great as Joanie kept saying."

Oh, please God, no. "Does she know, too?" Mom's pity would be intolerable.

Cynthia bit her lip. "I haven't said anything. Neither has Maddie. I think she's guessed, though. Are you very sad, being back here again?"

She sounded wistful, and DeeDee's heart twisted.

"I miss New York, but I'm happy to be near my family again, Cyn. I needed the change. Working with Mark is certainly... different."

Uncomfortable, too. Challenging.

She thought of her triumph at getting Mark outside, willingly, with her. His joy at earning the single truffle afterward.

Isaac's surprise at Mark's compliance.

The pride that had tickled her at the accomplishment.

Cynthia reached out and patted DeeDee's hand. "It agrees with you, DeeDee. You look great. I mean, you always do, but now... you're more relaxed."

"You're only saying that because you're an exemplary human being, overflowing with the milk of sisterly kindness. Speaking of which, can I get you a hot chocolate?" Anything to get back to the subject at hand. "Maybe it'll settle your stomach. Maddie says it cures everything."

Cynthia narrowed her eyes at the copper pot behind the counter, from which the most delicious aroma of cocoa and vanilla emanated.

DeeDee took a small sip of her own cocoa, wishing she hadn't ordered it because now that she'd tried it, there'd be no going back. "It must have a million calories. But oh man, it's so worth it."

Cynthia chewed the corner of her lip for a moment, then sighed. "I'd love one, but I better stick to herbal tea. So, about our problem."

Problems, plural, as it turned out. DeeDee set down her mug and looked over Cynthia's notes, wondering what on earth she'd gotten herself into.

Or rather, how Cynthia had thought pretzels and soda would be sufficient refreshments at a fashion show. Pregnancy brain? Lack of experience? This would never work.

"Fundraisers like this should be elegant," she explained. "There ought to be small plates of beautifully designed finger foods. Champagne or signature cocktails to drink. Spring flower arrangements on the tables. The whole event should be a decadent, indulgent, beautiful experience."

"But it's a fundraiser. If we spend all our money on refreshments and decorations, we're defeating our purpose."

DeeDee's mind raced. "What designers are you working with?"

Cynthia smiled. "It's not that kind of show, DeeDee. We're getting clothes from local retailers, evening wear from the bridal salon, and everything else from Copper Mountain Chic. It's a shop run by Sandra Reynolds; you'll love her. The woman oozes style. And she's as nice as she is beautiful, too. She's thrilled to be participating."

"I'm sure. Okay, that takes the pressure off. Haute-couture events require a certain élan. In Marietta, though, we can keep things simple." She jotted some notes.

Cynthia lifted one eyebrow. "Do you mean to be condescending?"

DeeDee looked up. "No. I'm just stating facts. What kind of garments are you showing?"

"Everything." Cynthia shrugged. "We want to make this accessible. Work clothing to business attire to prom and bridesmaid dresses, all for ordinary people with average bank accounts."

This was like no fashion show DeeDee had ever been

involved in. But all the better. It wouldn't take much to impress their benefactors and encourage them to open their pockets for Building Tomorrow.

"We still need refreshments," Deedee said. "Have you considered asking the Graff Hotel to contribute appetizers?"

"Even their discounted rate is too high." Cynthia grimaced. "I was going to ask Sage to contribute chocolate, but she's already run off her feet with Easter orders, I can't add another thing to her to-do list. I know she's been trying to squeeze in a baby shower for Portia, too." She slapped a hand over her mouth, looked cautiously over at the counter, then wilted with relief. "Thank goodness Dakota's working today. I can't believe this pregnancy brain. I've never ruined a surprise party before, and I definitely don't want to do it this time." She put her head in her hand.

"Is it a surprise?" DeeDee asked. Maddie had mentioned that Sage's niece wasn't comfortable talking about her condition. Surprise parties were tricky. In this case, it seemed like a disaster in the making, but that was for Sage to sort out.

"I don't know, but regardless, I can't ask anything more of Sage." She swallowed. "Now, there's something else. It's about the m-models. I ran into a little... s-s-snag."

DeeDee glanced up. The stutter was a bad sign. "What do you mean, a snag?"

"Well..." Cynthia was looking green again. "My plan was to contact Maya..."

"Maya Parrish? She's still in business? I can't believe a tiny local agency like hers could survive out here."

"She's Maya Gallagher now." Cynthia held up a palm, her eyes closed. She pressed a knuckle against her top lip, closed her eyes, and breathed deeply for a moment. "And it's hardly a tiny local agency. She runs a thriving headhunting firm for models and photographers. It is Internet based, so she has clients all over."

A surge of dread rippled through DeeDee's own stomach.

Overflowing with hubris, DeeDee had refused to consult the former model for career advice before flying off to New York, considering her own ambitions far loftier than that of someone who'd settled in Marietta, Montana.

"But I left it too late," Cynthia continued. "None of Maya's people are available. She thought she might have one or two, but even those didn't pan out."

"One or two models? You'll need at least a dozen to keep the show rolling."

This would never work.

"A dozen? Oh dear. Maybe you could talk to Maya yourself? Ask for some suggestions? Can't you play some kind of professional-courtesy card?"

Yeah, ask Jon how DeeDee played that game.

"Trust me, that'll only make things worse." She sighed. "There's a slight chance I may have hurt Maya's feelings when I left town."

"Huh." Cynthia dabbed at her forehead. Her lips had gone pale again. "Hurt in a you-didn't-compliment-my-coffee sort of way, or in a you-set-fire-to-my-car kind of way?"

"No actual flames." DeeDee wrinkled her nose. "Though there was a bridge-burning element to it."

"You insulted her business, didn't you?" Cynthia closed her eyes, breathing shallowly. "This is b-b-bad."

DeeDee studied her mug. "You make it sound so ugly. It was more like... friendly ribbing between rivals."

No. The exchange had been one sided, a careless display of ignorance from someone too blind to recognize the touch of a helping hand.

Cynthia's chair scraped backward as she jumped up, a hand over her mouth. "Excuse me," she muttered, fleeing to the washroom.

"I know the feeling," DeeDee said to the empty chair. A fashion show with no models. Could things get any worse?

The bell above the door jingled.

"DeeDee!"

She looked up to see the wide-eyed, ecstatic face of Mark Litton, attached to his large, clumsy body as it barreled straight toward her.

"Mark, wait!" Isaac reached for his brother. But it was too late.

Mark's jacket slipped through Isaac's fingers, leaving him grasping at air as he watched his brother rush toward the delicate corner table where Deirdre sat.

Crap.

"DeeDee!" Mark yelled. "You're here, you're here!"

"Watch the floor; it's wet." The girl behind the counter wore an orangey apron over a deep blue shirt with her dark hair carefully braided away from her face.

And yes, the freshly mopped floor was slippery. Isaac was close, but not close enough to catch his brother as he ran past the yellow plastic warning sign. Mark's running shoes, slick from their walk in the damp park, spun out beneath him and propelled him into Deirdre's chair, knocking her over and sending her mug of hot chocolate flying onto the floor.

Isaac bit back a curse.

"Whoa!" She tumbled backward and landed on her butt, legs splayed, her caramel-colored hair falling over her face. A button from her blouse flew off and bounced against the wall with a ping.

With a yelp, Mark landed heavily next to her.

Isaac was at his side in an instant, concern sharpening his voice. "Mark, are you okay? How many times must I tell you to slow down! Did you hit your head?"

Mark didn't deal well with injuries. His pain threshold was low, and he hated hospitals.

"No. My butt and my arm."

He held up his arm as if it were broken.

"Come on, buddy. You're okay." Isaac helped Mark to his feet. He'd stopped by the chocolate shop in hopes of getting to know more people in Marietta, but this was not the impression he'd hoped to make.

"I sorry, Isaac," Mark cried. "I sorry, DeeDee."

Deirdre pressed her hands against the floor, bringing her knees together and pushing her back against the wall. The blouse gaped, and Isaac could see the sparkling pink lace of her bra peeking out from the opening.

"No worries," she said faintly, "but next time, how about a handshake?"

She was breathing hard, the movement making the fabric gape and flutter.

Isaac yanked his gaze away, righted the chairs, and pushed Mark into one of them. "Stay there," he instructed.

Mark complied, but his breath was hitching in a telltale way that warned of an impending outburst.

"Sorry, Isaac. Sorry, sorry, sorry," he wailed. One pant leg was streaked from the damp floor and hiked up to reveal mismatched socks. His hair was sticking up at the back and falling into his eyes at the front. His glasses were askew.

A small crowd had formed around them, blocking the doorway to the shop. Isaac cringed at the kind but curious strangers. No doubt they meant well, but he wished he could send them all away and shield Mark from the embarrassment and humiliation.

Isaac had wanted to build some relationships before everyone saw how difficult things could be with Mark. It was why he'd pulled out of the Valentine Quest at the last minute. The February event had sounded like a fun way to become familiar with their new hometown, not to mention the awesome grand prize of a vacation.

But when he'd looked over the tasks involved, he knew Mark wasn't ready.

Coward. You were the one who wasn't ready.

An attractive redhead pushed her way through the huddle of onlookers. "What happened? Is anyone hurt? Dakota, get some towels, please. And the first aid kit. Should I call 911?"

"My brother slipped and crashed into Deirdre's table."

Isaac extended his hand to Dierdre, keeping his eyes on her face and avoiding the bounty in his peripheral vision. "Are you all right? I apologize about this."

Her breasts were small, firm, and perfectly proportioned, her skin satiny smooth, creamy, with the lightest dusting of freckles.

"I'm fine." She took his hand and let him help her up. "You guys sure know how to make an entrance."

Another woman appeared, blond and pale. "DeeDee, what happened?"

Isaac wanted to fall through the floor. He opened his mouth to explain, but Deirdre preempted him with a light touch to Mark's shoulder and a calm smile for the people surrounding them. "It seems this handsome dude and I are falling for each other. Literally." She ruffled Mark's hair, earning a wobbly smile. "Everything's okay. Back to your regularly programmed lives, people. Nothing to see here."

The onlookers chuckled and dispersed. Sniffling, Mark lifted a hand to the spot Deirdre had stroked. Isaac's eyebrows rose. Mark was a cuddly guy, but he didn't allow many people to touch his head.

"DeeDee." The blonde pointed to Deirdre's front and whispered, "Wardrobe malfunction alert."

Deirdre glanced down. "Will you look at that?"

"This is a family store, DeeDee," the redhead said with a laugh. "Let's keep the focus on the chocolate displays, okay?"

Appearing completely at ease, Deirdre tugged the edges of her shirt together. "Chocolate and entertainment. Sage, your customers got a bonus today."

Warmth rushed into Isaac's belly, low and heavy, as Deirdre's fingers trailed down the exposed skin of her chest. He was very glad she hadn't hurt herself, that only the garment had been damaged. It would be a crime to mar such smooth skin... He imagined pressing his lips to that silky cleft...

"Excuse me," Deirdre said wryly. She arranged her scarf to cover the opening in her top.

Isaac yanked his gaze up.

"Isaac." Deirdre had a mischievous grin on her face. "Have you met Sage?"

"Um," he said. Busted.

He shook hands with Sage Carrigan, the concerned red-head who owned the store, and the blonde, Cynthia Henley, Deirdre's stepsister. The clerk sopping up the mess with paper towels was Dakota.

"Good to meet you both," Dakota said.

"I'm glad everyone's okay." Sage looked at Mark, who was still blubbering softly. "How about a round of hot chocolate for the four of you, on the house?"

"You don't have to do that," Isaac began. Both Sage and Dakota sounded genuine, but if anything, he ought to be paying for the disruption.

"It's okay," Deirdre said. "Cynthia and I were finished anyway."

"Chocolate?" Mark swiped the back of his hand across his face. "Is this the magic chocolate store?"

"After yesterday," Isaac explained, "we had to come see for ourselves. We'll get out of your way."

Cynthia gave Isaac a speculative look. "Don't be silly. We can spare a few minutes, DeeDee."

"Good!" Sage said. "I love introducing people to Copper Mountain Chocolates. We make everything by hand here, and my hot chocolate is a special secret recipe."

Sage led them to a new table as Dakota finished cleaning up the spill.

"Secret?" Mark was enthralled, his upset forgotten. "I like secrets. And I'm special, too."

"Yes, you are, Mark," Dakota added. "You guys are in

for a treat. Here at Copper Mountain Chocolates, we like to say this is what love tastes like." She waved her hand to encompass the steaming copper kettle and the display cases filled with chocolate delicacies.

What love tastes like?

"That's a lot of pressure to put on a flavor." Isaac smiled. Mark's mood had done a complete one-eighty, so who was he to argue?

Sage prepared the beverages and handed them around.

Isaac lifted his mug to his lips. Suddenly, the tagline seemed one-hundred-percent appropriate. The aroma was deep, a little smoky almost, drifting upward with the steam. The mound of whipped cream tickled his tongue, melting along with the sip of the rich, silky, not-too-sweet beverage. And the chocolate itself, well... It was, in a word, perfect.

His eyes met Deirdre's across the table. She was watching him carefully, as if unaware of her own unguarded features. She hadn't accepted any cocoa, claiming she'd already had hers, and Isaac guessed again that she didn't often allow herself indulgences like this. What he saw in her face was yearning, unmet need, like a cold, hungry child pressing wistfully up against the window to a meal she couldn't join.

"Sure I can't get you one?" he offered.

She started, blinking, and then the expression disappeared. "No, thank you. I'm fine. Good, isn't it?"

She looked away, her cheeks growing pink.

Was she yearning for the hot chocolate?

Or was she yearning for... something else?

Chapter Eight

DEEDEE WASN'T SURE where the sudden awkwardness with Isaac had come from. So, he'd seen her bra—big deal. She'd changed clothes in front of entire camera crews dozens of times with no one batting an eye.

Maybe that was it. She'd grown accustomed to invisibility. A strange irony, for a model, she supposed, but it made sense. The focus was on the clothing, not the body beneath. Was that why she'd grown dissatisfied with the job?

Was that what the photographers, buyers, and designers sensed in her? They needed that neutrality, that invisibility, to highlight their product. A model who distracted the eye did them no good.

Then again, as Jon had so clearly pointed out, she wasn't the easiest person to work with.

Cynthia, recovered from her earlier nausea and now in full sales mode, was pimping the fashion show to Isaac, hoping to get his financial support. Given that the show was to raise funds for a community program that would directly benefit Mark, DeeDee figured Cynthia had it in the bag.

When Isaac reached into his pocket and pulled out his checkbook, DeeDee exchanged a grin with her stepsister. Cynthia was amazing. Isaac looked pleased with himself, as well. It was no doubt a position he was very comfortable with—being a benefactor, the man with the money and the solutions. The guy people counted on for help.

"Isaac," DeeDee said, pointing to his lip, "you've got some cream."

He raised his eyebrows. "Is that right?" Then, without taking his eyes off hers, he ran his tongue over his mouth. "Better?"

Oh, Lordy.

His lips were full, firm but soft looking. That delicious scruff on his face no doubt had just the right amount of raspiness… She'd meant to derail his macho manliness a tad. Instead, she'd unleashed his full sexiness.

This wasn't good.

"Yes," she croaked. She tried to swallow, but her mouth was like sandpaper.

He pushed his mug of cocoa across the table. "Have a sip. It'll help."

DeeDee cleared her throat and shoved the mug back. "I'm good." She scratched the side of her nose. "It's very generous of you to help support the fundraiser. Thank you."

A slow smile blossomed over his rugged face. "You're welcome. We've taken up enough of your time, though. Mark, we've got to go home and feed your fish."

Mark, who'd been deeply involved in getting every last drop of hot chocolate from his mug, lifted his sticky face and thought for a moment. "My fishies are hungry?"

"Yup."

"Okay." Mark got up. "Bye, DeeDee. Bye, Cinta. Bye, Sage. Bye, Kadoka. I have to feed my fishies."

When the bell on the door tinkled behind them, DeeDee slumped against her chair.

"Well, that was interesting." Cynthia crossed her arms and leaned back in her chair, raising a speculative eyebrow. "Wanna tell me how long that's been going on?"

"What?" DeeDee protested. "Nothing's going on. I work for him. I look after his brother. You're delusional."

From behind the counter, Dakota piped up. "I felt the heat from here. There's definitely something going on."

DeeDee put her head in her hands. "No, no, no. There isn't. There can't be. I work for him. He's rich, serious, and totally settled here. I'm broke, rudderless, and only in Marietta because I have nowhere else to go."

Silence. She looked up. "Wait. I didn't mean that the way it sounded."

Cynthia bit her lip and glanced over at Dakota and, darn it, Sage, who stood at the entrance to the workroom where she made her chocolates.

They'd all clearly heard the disparaging remark. People who lived in Marietta loved Marietta, and DeeDee knew better than to speak ill of it. She hadn't meant to—it had just slipped out. But it was a big reason not to get involved with someone who lived here.

"We wondered," Sage said. "I'm so sorry things haven't gone well for you."

To DeeDee's surprise, Sage's tone was filled with so much kindness that it brought heat to the back of her throat.

Oh, God. Again, she put her hand to her mouth. She was such an idiot. Yes, she, who had no social collateral to waste, had just dissed her hometown to three very loyal residents.

But even worse, she'd accidentally admitted that she, the big New York City model, was a fake, a fraud.

A complete failure.

"Ha-ha." It was a pathetic attempt. Her stomach twisted. "Cat's out of the bag now, isn't it? Can't wait until Carol Bingley gets hold of this tidbit. Everyone will have a good laugh at Deirdre Cash, who thought she was too big for little old Marietta." She got to her feet, clutching her bag. "I need to go. Thanks for... thanks."

Sage gripped her forearm. "Sit down, you giant baby." But there was fondness in her tone. "So, it's your turn to churn the gossip mill for a bit. You'll survive. I've been there. So has Cynthia."

"We all have," Dakota added. "No one's judging you. Well, not everyone's judging you." She smiled.

"Not helping." DeeDee flopped her head into her hands. Then she looked up. "You've all got stories?"

Sage made a face. "Dawson's jealous ex came after me with a gun. When I was in bed with him."

It was a legendary story that couldn't have been easy to live down.

"Remember my *Famous Interview*?" Cynthia cocked an eyebrow at her.

Cynthia always referred to it in a voice that made it sound like it was in capital letters. Her *Famous Interview* about the business climate in Marietta. Except she hadn't said climate. She'd said climax.

The interview had gone viral.

DeeDee had laughed as hard as anyone at that. Poor shy, stuttering Cynthia.

"And don't forget Leah Morgan," Sage added.

Lonely Leah, as she'd been dubbed by the reality TV show that had nearly ruined her, had referred to Marietta as a backwater town in the middle of nowhere. While drunk.

On national television.

"I guess if the town can forgive that, there's hope for me," DeeDee said.

"Turns out there was a lot more to the story," Sage said. "We've all had stuff happen. Sure, sometimes we laugh at each other, but we always support each other in the long run."

That sounded good. Really, really good. But it didn't apply to her. DeeDee hadn't ever really been there for anyone, long run or short. She knew what she deserved. It was time to shut up and take it.

And one way or another, she was going to save Cynthia's show.

ISAAC COULDN'T GET that bare half-smile of creamy flesh, like a lacy wink, out of his mind. Deirdre had stared at him as if she could read his mind and hear the blood rushing through his veins, daring him to look away while she casually covered herself.

The woman seemed impervious to embarrassment.

It had been a long time since Isaac had been stirred like this by a woman's body. And never under these circumstances. That he'd glimpsed her breasts and silky lingerie in a public place, surrounded by strangers, added an element of the forbidden to the encounter.

The fact that she worked for him only made it worse.

Isaac had had every intention of pretending it hadn't happened, of putting it out of his mind, but the very next morning, while she waited to pick Mark up for a routine appointment, she'd leaned against the doorframe, stretched like a cat, gave him a heavy-lidded smile, and then winked.

Isaac had lost his train of thought, lost his voice, hell, lost his mind.

He'd gotten almost nothing done after that. Before he knew it, the front door crashed open, and Mark's lumbering footsteps sounded, followed by Deirdre's lighter tread.

Might as well say hi.

Isaac met them upstairs. "Did you have a good check-up?" Finding a doctor Mark liked had been a huge relief.

"I'm hungry, DeeDee," Mark said, ignoring him. "Will you have cookies with me? And play checkers?"

From his mouth, it sounded like chiggers.

"It's up to your brother, Markie." Deirdre punched Mark lightly in the shoulder. "His wish is my command. And jackets live in closets, not on floors."

Mark blinked and shoved his glasses up his nose. "What?"

"Pick up your jacket." Isaac heard the snap in his voice and took a beat. Of course Mark was focused more on Deirdre. It was what Isaac wanted. "Help Deirdre clean for thirty minutes, then you can have one cookie."

Mark's forehead puckered as his lip began to quiver. "But, Isaac—"

Isaac wanted to kick himself.

"Or," Deirdre said, shooting Isaac a meaningful glance, "we'll have a healthy snack and then go for a walk so I can tell you about the doctor's visit."

"Yay!" Mark yelled. Then, "I don't wanna walk."

Isaac had been thinking about Deirdre for hours, but now that she was here, he was annoyed. With her, with Mark.

With himself.

"I wanna have cookies. And watch TV." Mark stuck his

lower lip out and crossed his arms.

"Deirdre is getting you a snack." He didn't have time for one of Mark's meltdowns today. Since Deirdre was such a hero in Mark's eyes, she could deal with the fallout. "I've got some calls to make. I'll hear the doctor's report after that."

"Aye, aye, Mr. Litton, sir." Deirdre touched two fingers to her temple in salute.

"Aye, aye," Mark echoed, grabbing her arm. "Come on, DeeDee."

"Where do jackets live?" Deirdre asked, pointing to Mark's huge varsity-style bomber.

This time, Mark laughed, catching on. "In closets. Not on floors. It's a joke, right?"

"Yup. You know what to do."

Mark picked up his things without grumbling.

Isaac listened to Mark and Deirdre's cheerful chatter, a departure from the usual canned laugh-track of television sitcoms he'd become accustomed to hearing at this time of day. And hated.

"No sweets," Isaac called as he descended to his office. The door closed upstairs without a response.

He looked at his touch screen but didn't make a move to initiate the call.

Contrary to any reasonable expectations, Deirdre was turning out to be more of a companion to his brother than anyone he'd hired in the past. She didn't treat Mark like an idiot, a patient, or a problem. She treated Mark like... a person.

She was exactly what he wanted for Mark.

And triggered an attraction that he wanted to avoid, for himself.

Oh well. He hit the button to connect with his client. There were worse things.

Thirty minutes later, just as he completed his call, Deirdre and Mark clomped down the stairs to Isaac's office. She carried a plate of apple slices, cheddar cheese, and crackers to the table by the window.

"Figured you could use a snack, too." She arched an eyebrow at him.

She'd changed into a jogging suit that emphasized her perfect curves. He pretended not to notice.

"DeeDee says low blood sugar makes you crabby," Mark said. "We have to eat fruit and veg'tables. And cheese is okay sometimes too, but not too much. 'Cuz of the fat and clesstrol. Right, DeeDee?"

"That's right, Markie-Mark. Go get your running shoes on while I tell Isaac what they said at the clinic."

〜

"GOOD NEWS, I hope?" He'd enrolled Mark in a heart-smart program as soon as they'd moved, but he'd been inconsistent in implementing the advice.

"Excellent news," Deirdre said. "He's doing great. He's lost four pounds, his blood pressure is down a point or two, and perhaps you're not aware, but he runs up those stairs like a gazelle."

"A herd of gazelles, maybe." He smiled.

Deirdre buffed her nails on her sleeve. "Thank you, DeeDee. You've done a fantastic job, DeeDee. How can I express my appreciation, DeeDee? A raise? Of course! A car? Why not?"

The tension at the back of his scalp eased. She was fun to have around. Good for Mark, good company, easy on the eyes. As long as they kept it at that, things would be fine.

"He seems happy," he said.

"He's got a gift for happiness," she responded. "He's lucky that way."

"Not a lot of people would call my brother lucky."

She shrugged. "A lot of people call me lucky. Goes to show what they know."

He cocked his head. "And aren't you? I thought being a model was every little girl's dream."

She blinked, then pushed away from the wall. Her expression had closed. He wasn't sure what that meant. She wasn't a happy person or she hadn't enjoyed modeling?

But before he could question her further, Mark was back, decked out in his sweatpants and running shoes.

"And we're off," Deirdre said with a nod. "See you in an hour, Isaac."

"Wait!" Mark said. "First, I want to show you my fishes!"

Deirdre rolled her eyes good-naturedly as Mark took her

arm and brought her to the first tank.

Isaac never would have guessed that she'd have so much patience.

"These are called tetras." Mark pronounced the word carefully, going on to tell Deirdre their names and their personalities, as well as how old they were, which ones liked which others, and all sorts of other details that washed over Isaac like rain.

Mark's ability to memorize never failed to amaze him. His mother had given birth to Mark when she was forty-two. Isaac was nine at the time and accustomed to being the only child. He recognized his baby brother was different, but he didn't understand why his mother was crying and why his father refused to hold his new son.

Their muttered arguments and icy silences continued after Mark's birth. Before the baby's first birthday, Dad was gone, abandoning not just the handicapped child who'd have no memories of him, but also his overwhelmed wife and Isaac, who knew if he just tried hard enough, worked hard enough at school, he could be smart for both him and his brother.

Deirdre spoke, breaking into Isaac's memories.

"They're very pretty fish. It looks like you take very good care of them, Mark."

Mark adored animals and desperately wanted a dog or a cat. Isaac found the fish to be plenty of work and was pleased they seemed to satisfy this need in his brother.

"Oh no, not me." Mark took Deirdre's hand and stroked it. "I love my fishes, but I could do it wrong and make them die. Sometimes, I can't be trusted."

Isaac's head snapped up. "Who told you that, Mark?"

If someone at the care home had been picking on him or belittling him, they'd find themselves on the wrong end of a lawsuit. No one hurt his little brother, not while Isaac was in charge.

Mark smiled at him. "You did, Isaac." Then he nodded at Deirdre in confirmation. "I do dumb stuff sometimes. Isaac is pertecting me."

The simple words coming from his brother's mouth ran through Isaac like a hot knife. "I've never... I would never... Mark, you know I wouldn't—"

"Easy there, Ike," Deirdre interrupted. "If your face gets any redder, it'll pop like a tomato in the microwave. Mark knows you love him. He probably just overheard you talking to someone else. It's no big deal. Right, Mark?"

"I know Ike loves me," Mark said.

Ike.

Isaac's jaw ached.

"And it's kind of true anyway, right?" she continued. "There are things you shouldn't be trusted with. I mean, you do ride the short bus, bud."

Rippling heat galvanized Isaac's tongue. "You did *not* just say that."

But instead of being angry or hurt, Mark laughed. "It's

not a short bus, DeeDee. It's a reg'lar bus. But it's full of special people. My friend Abe fell on his head when he was two, so now he's special. My other friend Paulie got born too early, and he's special. And not just his brain. His legs are special sometimes, too. I like special people. And I'm lucky that Isaac looks after me. He's the very best brother in the whole world. I love you so much!"

Mark threw his chubby arms around Isaac's waist, and all the outrage melted away. He put his arms around his brother and patted his back, blindingly aware that Deirdre was watching them. He did not tolerate snide comments about Mark, whether the boy was around to hear or not.

It stung to realize that he himself was guilty of the same thing. What other thoughtless remarks had Mark overheard him say?

"I'm sorry, Mark. I didn't mean to hurt you."

Mark tipped his face up. So much love and trust shone from his eyes that Isaac's heart twisted in his chest.

"You never hurt me. You love me."

Isaac nodded, his throat too tight to speak.

Then Deirdre touched his shoulder. "Don't feel bad, Isaac. He knows you love him. Now, you didn't tell me whether these fish get scrambled eggs or toast for supper. Or maybe you share your oatmeal with them in the morning. Is that it, Marco Polo?"

"I'm not Marco Polo!" Mark giggled. "And fish don't eat oatmeal or scrambled eggs or toast. They eat… What's that stuff called, Isaac?"

"Fish flakes." The conversation was spinning out of control.

"Like corn flakes," Mark crowed, "but for fish! Come on, DeeDee, I'll show you where they are."

"We'll feed the fish and then we're going for our walk, right?"

"Okay." With a sigh, Mark pushed away from Isaac and led Deirdre to the cupboard beneath the first tank, where the supplies were kept. The kid—he'd always be Isaac's kid brother—was chattering like a chipmunk, overjoyed at the attention, and not only was he not upstairs watching television, but he'd had an apple instead of cookies.

Deirdre looked over her shoulder as Mark pulled out the plastic containers of fish food. Isaac braced himself for some snarky remark, but instead, she gave him a hesitant, almost apologetic smile.

She wasn't feeling sorry for him, was she?

He swallowed. He didn't need her pity. He didn't need her censure or whatever advice she, in her ignorance, deemed necessary.

He watched as she rested her hand lightly on his brother's back, patting and comforting. She had long, pretty fingers.

He exhaled heavily. He hadn't wanted her. He didn't need her. But she was proving remarkably difficult to ignore.

Chapter Nine

"HELLO, KNOCK, KNOCK." Deirdre pushed open the door to Isaac's office. Mark's head bobbed around the side of her shoulder. He was trying unsuccessfully to hide a grin.

They were up to something, and Isaac found this unaccountably annoying. It was great to see Mark engaged and occupied, rather than bored and lonely, but Isaac hadn't expected Mark finding a new favorite person would bother him so much.

He felt left out, which made no sense. Deirdre was doing exactly what he'd asked, and more. He should be thrilled. Mom was thrilled; on her latest check in—from the British Virgin Islands—Mark had told her all about Deirdre. Their mom had cried from missing them, but he'd heard relief and gratitude, too.

"Yes. Is there something you need?"

Her eyebrows went up. Her smile faded, as did Mark's.

"First," she said, "you can remove the outgrowth of xylem and phloem from your coccygeal region. Then you can give me your car keys and credit card."

He blinked and frowned. "What?"

Mark burst into peals of laughter. "Take the stick out of your butt, Isaac!" He stepped back and gave Deirdre a high-five. "She said it fancy so you wouldn't know! You had 'sylum and phlegm in your costly region!"

"How long have you been holding that one?" he asked drily.

Deirdre grinned. "It occurred to me on the spur of the moment. Don't look so shocked. I took Biology 101. Incidentally, Mark needs new clothes. Based on his current wardrobe, I propose you let me choose his next one."

"Mark doesn't need new clothes."

"A dog scratched my pants," Mark said.

"We stopped in at the animal shelter the other day," Deirdre explained. "I'm not sure who was more excited, Mark or the dogs."

Isaac could just imagine.

"They're holey," Mark added. "But not the cool kind of holes."

Since when was Mark concerned about cool anything?

"Do they still cover your… coccygeal region?"

He tried not to think about that portion of DeeDee's anatomy, the way her slacks clung to those curves.

Then he thought of her other curves, and the pink spar-kles on the bra he'd seen when she'd fallen in the chocolate shop.

Had it been only a couple of weeks?

Mark put his hands over his mouth, delighted. "That means my butt."

"He's got a closet-full of clothes," Isaac said. "He doesn't need anything else." He pushed aside the memory of Mark's shabby appearance in the chocolate shop that day.

Deirdre's nostrils flared gently. "Isaac, are you aware of the stratification that occurs whenever a group gathers together?"

"Stratification? What are you talking about?" He glanced at Mark, but the boy only nodded earnestly, as if he understood her completely.

Deirdre pursed her lips. "There's a social cost involved with falling into the... lower levels," she continued, keeping her voice even. "This often occurs on a subconscious level, based on superficial impressions. I'd like to ensure that a certain character we're both invested in does not suffer such effects." She paused. "You picking up what I'm laying down?"

"I take issue with what you're laying down." He turned to Mark. "I need a glass of water. Would you go get me one please, please?"

"'kay, Isaac," Mark said, heading for the stairs. "See you later, alligator."

"In a while, crocodile," he responded.

The second Mark disappeared, Isaac spoke. "Are you telling me that people are judging Mark based on his clothes?"

"It's more than clothing. Everyone gets judged based on their appearance," Deirdre said, crossing her arms. "We assess people in the blink of an eye, without being aware of it. Age, confidence, social status, a million little things."

Isaac's jaw hurt. Red tinged the edges of his vision. "You're a model. I understand clothing is important to you. But Mark doesn't care as long as he's comfortable. Image isn't everything, Deirdre."

She flinched, but recovered quickly. "It's not nothing either. It's easy to say image isn't important when you've got exactly the image that everyone wants."

She stopped and caught her breath. Color rode high on her cheekbones. "Mark wears jeans and sweatshirts all the time, which wouldn't be that bad, but now that he's trimming down, his pants are barely hanging on. His tennis shoes need replacing, too."

Isaac ordered Mark's stuff online. It saved them both a lot of grief. But maybe he'd fallen behind.

"I don't mean to be critical," Deirdre said, "but an updated image could give your brother an edge in his world, okay? He's got enough strikes against him; he doesn't need more."

Her chest was rising and falling quickly, and the passion in her voice was mesmerizing.

"What do you want me to do?" He lifted his arms helplessly. "He despises shopping even more than I do. It's a battle. We just end up exhausted and mad."

DeeDee's face softened. "Let me do it. I know what I'm looking for, I know where to go, and I know how to make it as quick and painless as possible. I might not have a lot of skills, Isaac, but trust me, I know how to shop."

A smile tugged at his lips. "I do believe that."

"And can I please take him for a haircut? Honestly, Isaac, it looks like you cut it yourself using a bowl and kitchen shears."

"He doesn't like people touching his head," he said. "Which makes haircuts tricky."

"Then he needs a new hairdresser."

He grudgingly admitted that there was some sense to her words.

Mark arrived, a dripping glass of water in his hands. "Here, Isaac. I got it."

"Thanks, bro." Isaac took a sip, met Deirdre's eyes over the rim of the glass, and felt a subtle agreement pass between them.

"A couple of hours and he'll be a new man," she said. "I'll need your credit card and your car keys."

"What's wrong with your car?"

She widened her eyes and glanced sideways at Mark. "Your car is more comfortable."

Ah, yes. The little import she drove was not designed for someone of Mark's build. He appreciated that she'd not drawn attention to the fact.

"Of course." He took his keys from the dish on his desk

and tossed them to her, then handed her his card. "I'll see you when you get back. Have fun. If that's possible."

She smiled back. "Trust me, Ike. Your brother is in good hands with me."

After touching his arm briefly, she went to join Mark in the car.

She really did care about Mark, he realized. There was a genuine, thoughtful, real woman beneath the pretty packaging, one who appealed to him, and not just on the physical level.

She'd asked him to trust her.

Could he do that?

THEY'D HAD WONDERFUL luck, as it turned out. DeeDee had made sure to get Mark a snack, a healthy green smoothie filled with vegetables and just enough fruit to satisfy his sweet tooth. She'd taken him to Livingston, where there was a wider variety of stores, and had found some great sales.

After that, she'd taken him to the stylist Maddie recommended. It was amazing what a difference the right haircut made. Isaac would be so impressed.

She pulled up to the house and parked Isaac's car. She was tired of driving borrowed vehicles, but this one was a treat.

"I'm tired, DeeDee." Mark yawned loudly. "Can I watch TV when we get inside?"

"I'm guessing Isaac's going to want to see what we bought. Would you like to model your new clothes for him?"

"No. Can I show him tomorrow?"

Perhaps she'd pushed him hard enough.

"Tell you what. Go say hi, let him see your new 'do, and then you can go watch TV. Deal?"

"Deal," he replied.

He slumped through the door and she followed, her arms laden with packages.

"Isaac, we're home," Mark shouted. "Come see my new 'do."

Isaac came out of his office and did an immediate double-take. "Why is Brad Pitt standing in my doorway? DeeDee, what did you do with my brother?"

The fatigue on Mark's face immediately vanished.

DeeDee's heart swelled, and she put a hand to her chest. Isaac was such a dork sometimes, but when it came to his brother, he could really pull it out of the weeds when he wanted to.

"It's me, Mark. Your brother." Mark poked at Isaac. "I got a haircut, and I didn't hate it."

Isaac glanced at DeeDee, his brows raised. "Is that so? I'm happy to hear it. You were starting to look a little shaggy around the edges."

"I was not! You're shaggy!"

Who knew that wrestling and tussling with his handicapped brother could make a guy seem so hot?

"You like your new clothes, don't you, Mark? Are you sure you wouldn't like to show them off for your brother?"

"No," Mark said. "I hate changing clothes."

"All right," she said. "Thanks for a fun afternoon, Marco."

"Thank you for helping me shop, DeeDee," Mark called, already focused on the television.

"You're welcome, Marcus. Any day."

He giggled as she'd expected. "My name is Mark!"

"Okay, Marco Polo. Whatever you say."

"Mark!"

"Market?" she called after him. "Marksman? Marvelous? Marsupial?"

Isaac pulled her into the dining room. "He's about at his limit, DeeDee. Though I confess, I've never seen him have such a good time with someone who teases him as much as you do. It's mystifying."

She shrugged. "I'm a girl who knows how to get the best out of people."

"You're a natural salesperson. I suppose that makes sense, with the modeling. What's that if not selling? Women are frighteningly open to being told of their deficiencies."

DeeDee thought about Jon, always finding fault, never satisfied.

Isaac touched the knuckle of his forefinger to her upper arm. "So let me be the one to say you're doing an amazing job, DeeDee."

Chapter Ten

A FEW DAYS later, DeeDee set aside the meal plan she was compiling for Mark and glanced at her cell phone. Ten minutes until he got home. She got to her feet and went to the refrigerator for the salad veggies.

Mark had accepted the dietary improvements. He no longer argued about the daily walks, either. His endurance had improved and he wasn't huffing so much at the hilly spots, which meant it was working. Sage's chocolates were a powerful incentive.

The activity was working for her, too. Between the chocolate and Mom's care packages, she had to keep her metabolism revved. Fortunately, running up and down the stairs at Isaac's burned a lot of calories, leaving her with a surprisingly pleasant tiredness at the end of the day.

As she sliced into a tomato, a splat of juice escaped, landing on her jeans. She wiped it off, grateful she'd given in to Isaac's suggestion that she go casual when she was with Mark. She still did her hair and makeup, of course. She'd seen Isaac's look of male appreciation when her boobs had nearly made an appearance that day at the chocolate shop. While she didn't want to care what he thought, it felt good to be… well… appreciated.

Isaac's unexpected compliment after her shopping trip with Mark still warmed her. Though, as if to make up for it, he'd been preoccupied, distant, and demanding since then.

Her phone vibrated, indicating a text message. It was Isaac. From downstairs.

Isaac: *Don't forget, you're staying late tonight. Mark will need dinner.*

Yes, he'd told her about a dozen times. He had an important conference call that would go into the evening. She knew.

DeeDee: *Amazingly, I still haven't forgotten. There's a rotisserie chicken in the oven, and I'm making a salad right now. Also, it's creepy to text someone when you're in the same house.*

Maybe she should make some pasta, too. A small portion of carbs wouldn't be bad for Mark. She got out a pot and put the water on to heat.

Another buzz.

Isaac: *Thank you. And it's not creepy. It's efficient.*

She smiled. Isaac was all about efficiency. And order, despite the last stack of boxes remaining in the kitchen corner. She glanced around her. It was like a tornado blew the stuff in, and Isaac and Mark had simply opened doors and stepped aside. No wonder they had relied on takeout. It must drive Isaac nuts to be in here.

The water was just starting to simmer. She had time to unpack a box or two. Isaac would like that. Of course, he wouldn't have a clue where anything was. She thumbed back.

DeeDee: Maybe you prefer texting because you're afraid of me. I understand. I'm pretty intimidating.

The first box contained mostly dish towels, but also a box of toothpicks, a bag of brown sugar, and an impressive collection of still-wrapped chopsticks from a Chinese food place in Chicago.

DeeDee: Who packed for you? A chimp with ADD? I need a raise.

There was no order she could see in how the contents of the kitchen had been arranged, so she started moving things around.

Another buzz:

Isaac: Nice. My brother packed.

DeeDee's breath caught. Oh, God. She'd been joking. That must have sounded horrible.

She started fumbling out a response when another text came through.

Isaac: *Gotcha. Now who's scared? I'm busy. Quit distracting me.*

DeeDee heaved a sigh, then chuckled to herself. So, the stern Isaac had a playful side.

The water was almost boiling, and she readied the box of pasta when her phone buzzed again. She prepared to further the banter with Isaac, but caller ID showed that it was from Cynthia this time. It was a call, not a text.

"Hey, baby mama," she said, leaning against the counter, readying for a chat. She wasn't big into babies herself, but Cynthia was so stoked her excitement was contagious.

"Where are you?" It was Chad, not Cynthia.

"At Isaac's, waiting for Mark. Why?" She straightened up. "Where's Cynthia?"

"Hospital." Chad voice was wire tight.

"Hospital?" DeeDee's heart stuttered. "What... why... what happened?"

"She started bleeding. She asked me to call. Can you come?"

DeeDee turned off the stove before Chad had finished speaking. "I'll be right there."

Poor, sweet Cynthia.

She almost fell down the stairs in her haste, pushed open the door to Isaac's office, and stuck her head in.

He gave her a quick, distracted nod and held up his index finger, but she ignored it.

"Something came up. I have to leave." Her voice was

shaking.

Isaac spoke quickly into his headset and flicked the button to mute the call before turning to her. The half-smile faded. Deep lines bracketed his eyes and his hair was mussed, as if he'd been running his fingers through it.

"I specifically requested you to stay later tonight."

"Family emergency. No time to explain."

She shoved her phone into the front pocket of her bag and yanked on her coat. Last thing she wanted was for stoic Isaac Litton to see her cry. She ran out the door, ignoring his response. Rain had blown in with the brisk spring breeze, and she was going to get wet on the way to her car.

Cynthia had to be okay. She just had to.

Isaac reached the car a second behind her. He slapped his hand on the door, so she couldn't pull it open.

"What's going on, Deirdre? Mark will be home any minute, and I've got three clients on hold."

Tears stung her eyes, which made her furious.

"I know this is inconvenient for you, but you'll have to manage. Let Mark watch TV while you finish work. He's used to that, right?"

A muscle in his jaw flickered.

"You're upset."

"Yeah, I am." She dashed moisture off her cheek. "It's my stepsister. She's in the ER. Now, let me go."

She pushed past him, and this time, he let her.

"DID YOU KNOW Isaac was such a workaholic when you set me up with him? He's so self-absorbed." DeeDee paced the waiting room in the emergency department at the Marietta hospital, worry gnawing at her stomach.

"Says the woman working two jobs." Maddie was pacing an opposite path to DeeDee. She appeared somewhat less crazed, but it was a narrow margin as she was almost as excited about this baby as the parents-to-be.

"He doesn't get it that some people have actual lives."

"And you do?"

"Harsh, Maddie. Harsh."

On some level, DeeDee knew that her irritation at Isaac was out of proportion to his actions. But who else could she be angry at? Cynthia didn't deserve this. With her big, soft heart, she'd be devastated if something happened to her baby.

Dave, the ER nurse, poked his head out. "You can come in and see her now, if you like."

As they rushed him, he stuck his arms out sideways, like a scarecrow, nearly clotheslining them.

"Easy, you two. Geez. She needs peace and quiet and calm. Maddie? We've been down this road before. Can I trust you to behave yourself?"

Maddie threw him an exasperated look. "I believe I proved myself rather well the last time you and I butted heads."

"Well, this isn't a big, strong stranger with the hots for

you. This is your very frightened younger sister." Some very personal concern slipped through Dave's professional demeanor. Cynthia was well-loved in Marietta, as was Chad.

Maddie straightened her shoulders, nodding. "I know, Dave. Thanks. I appreciate you looking out for her."

He cleared his throat, then looked at DeeDee. "You'll keep this one in check, too?"

"Don't talk about me like I'm not here," DeeDee snapped. "Also, I don't need a handler."

Dave pursed his lips and crossed his arms. "If you say so."

DeeDee remembered that they'd gone to high school together. Uh-oh. Did he have a grudge against her?

"Did we date?" she asked.

He blew a puff of air through his lips. "Thank God, no. I was a dumb science nerd. You didn't go for guys like me."

But he'd asked, she thought. A dumb, *brave* science nerd. And the response she'd have given him was laughter. She and Maddie had enjoyed breaking hearts back then. Maddie, however, seemed to have redeemed herself in Dave's eyes.

DeeDee still had a long way to go.

"Look," she told him. "If I hurt you back then, I apologize. Can we let bygones be bygones?"

They looked at each other for a long moment, and she sensed the tension lift. They were grown-ups now.

"Water under the bridge," Dave said. "Besides, I was way too good for you."

Before she could respond, Maddie's arm landed on her shoulders. "We'll be good with Cynthia, Dave. The very definition of calm and controlled."

The sound of footsteps behind them caught Dave's attention. "All right, your parents are here. You two go comfort your sister while I talk to them. Five minutes."

Maddie reached for her hand, the same way she had when they were small. "She has to be okay," she said as they wound their way through the maze of curtained-off cubicles.

"She will be okay," DeeDee promised. She prayed she was right.

Then they saw her. Cynthia lay back on the narrow mattress, looking pale and thin against the pastel sheets. Chad sat in a chair next to her, holding her hand to his chest.

"Cynthia," DeeDee whispered.

Maddie was already crying.

"Hey, hey. Look who's here." Cynthia pushed with her elbows to sit up.

Chad got to his feet and kissed each of them on the cheek. "Thanks for coming."

Then he bent down to his fiancée and brushed her forehead with his hand. The simple gesture was so laden with tenderness that DeeDee's eyes welled up.

"I'll let you visit with your sisters for a few minutes. Okay, honey?"

Cynthia nodded, her eyes following his broad back as he walked away.

Maddie sat in Chad's chair while DeeDee dragged an unused one from a nearby cubicle. They didn't have much time before Dave returned, so Cynthia spoke quickly.

"I'm okay. The b-b-baby's alive."

Maddie heaved a shuddering sigh. "Oh, thank God."

"Or, rather," Cynthia said, her voice breaking. "I should s-s-say *one* of the babies is alive."

Chapter Eleven

"TWINS," DEEDEE SAID, clutching Maddie's hand again.

"I w-wanted it to be a surprise." Cynthia gulped back fresh tears. "I was so excited to tell your m-m-mom. To raise you two, and then have twin grandchildren…"

Dave came in then and shooed them all out so they could move Cynthia from the Emergency room to Maternity. The remaining twin was alive, but the doctors wanted to monitor her overnight, at least.

Maddie left to pick up Mick, who was just getting back from a trip to Alaska where he'd dropped off a party of eco-tourists. Their mom, torn between worry for Cynthia and Norm, finally chose to take her husband home, promising to return in the morning.

Suddenly, DeeDee was alone.

Once again, she was overwhelmed with the sense of being out of place, out of the loop, a newcomer in her own family, an outsider who'd once wanted nothing more than to get as far away from Montana as she could.

She'd done that, and look where it had gotten her. Right back where she'd started.

Dave walked up to her, the fatigue from a long shift showing in the lines on his face. "Cynthia's settled now and asking for you. I'll show you to her room."

She got to her feet, feeling creaky from too much time in vinyl upholstered chairs. "Does this mean you're done being mad at me?"

"High school was a long time ago, Stretch. And life's too short." He glanced back at her, a tired smile on his face. "Besides, after twelve hours on the job, I don't have the time or energy for anyone but my patients. If Cynthia's not mad at you, why should I be?"

His words humbled her. "Now you're just twisting the knife."

He led her to the elevator and pressed the button for Maternity. There was a wedding ring on his left hand, she observed.

"It's not about you, DeeDee." He evaluated her thoughtfully. "And if it was, well, I like where I'm at in my life."

She looked at the lights above the elevator door, feeling herself flush at the implication. Word had gotten around that her life wasn't the blazing success she'd let them believe.

In the time she'd been "finding herself" and having a good time, Dave had gotten a useful degree. He was using his skills to save lives and help people who were suffering. He'd gotten married, might even have a kid or two of his own.

It was no secret that DeeDee had accomplished none of these things. Her stomach spasmed, that old pain just below her ribs. Suddenly, her ambitions and disappointments seemed so petty, her problems nothing more than the insignificant obsessions of a spoiled princess.

The elevator dinged and the door opened.

"Down the hall, turn right. Third room on the left."

"Thanks, Dave."

He held the elevator door open until DeeDee walked through. Then, as it was closing, he added, "The main cafeteria's closed, but there's a vending machine at the end of the hall if you're hungry."

She pushed away the memories of her teenage self, the one who'd mocked boys like Dave and their hopeless crushes, flouncing about while tossing her hair in their faces.

The laughter was on the other foot now, wasn't it?

Whoever said you couldn't go home again had it right. Or perhaps as a returning heroine, you could.

Not so much when you were slinking back with your tail between your legs.

She straightened her shoulders. Where was this coming from? She wasn't prone to self-pity, or pity of any kind. Shaking off the mopes, she pushed open the door to Cynthia's room.

She looked a little better, not as shocked or frightened as she'd appeared in the ER. She had an IV line in one arm and some wires sticking out from under her hospital gown.

"Hey, babe." DeeDee tiptoed up to her stepsister's bed and perched on the chair at her side.

"DeeDee." Cynthia reached for her and began crying again. "I'm s-s-sorry, the hormones are making me leak like a s-sieve. It's awful."

The stutter that had bothered Cynthia throughout her life only appeared now when she was emotionally stressed. And this certainly counted as such a time.

DeeDee enfolded her, pressing Cynthia's head into her shoulder, stroking her golden hair, feeling the wracking sobs shudder through her, into her very bones. "You cry all you want, honey. This sucks, what's happening to you."

Cynthia wept and wept. Finally, she pushed away and sat back. She wiped a hand over her face. "It really does suck," she agreed in a tremulous voice. "B-but I'll be okay."

"Of course you will. You're so strong. You survived Maddie and me, after all. You can get through anything, right?"

"Oh, DeeDee," Cynthia said, gripping her hand. "I've missed you so much."

Guilt, shocking in its intensity, washed over DeeDee. She'd never expected that her absence would have mattered so much.

"Oh, honey. I'm here now. That's what matters."

"Yes, it does." Cynthia took a moment to compose herself. "I know you're working with Mark, but DeeDee, I need you more than ever now."

"And I'm here. The fundraiser is under control. Everything's going to be okay, Cyn."

Cynthia's eyes overflowed again. "The show is in two weeks, and I'm going to be on bedrest for who knows how long."

"I can handle the final details." She patted Cynthia's hand. "You're making yourself crazy."

"But now I need you to host it, too. Can you handle that? Being the emcee?"

DeeDee blinked. "Oh. Right."

She loved waltzing down the runway, and the few roles she'd played had been great fun.

But emceeing a show involved talking... as herself. People looking at her. Listening to her.

The *real* her.

"Isn't there anyone else?" she asked, a little desperately. Being real was not her strong suit.

"Chad and Eric will help out. Logan too, probably. But you're perfect for it, DeeDee. You're a real model, but you're one of us, too."

Not likely.

"And now," Cynthia added, "you're connected to the disability community through Mark and Isaac."

At the moment. This wasn't meant to be a long-term thing.

Not that she knew what her long-term thing was.

She glanced up. "I guess."

Cynthia eyed her curiously.

"What?" DeeDee asked at the look.

"You seem to have gotten attached to the Litton brothers."

"Mark thinks I hung the moon, and you know me and adoration." She snorted. "He is a sweetie, though."

"And Isaac? Is he a sweetie, too?"

That Cynthia could tease at all under the circumstances made DeeDee love her even more.

"He's okay." DeeDee shrugged, hoping Cynthia wouldn't see that her feelings about Isaac were much more complicated than that. "We get along."

Cynthia folded her arms. "Looked like a little more than that, the day in the chocolate shop."

"What a crazy thing to happen." DeeDee's cheeks grew warm. "It was pretty funny, wasn't it?"

"Isaac wasn't laughing. He looked as if he wanted to eat you up with a spoon."

Oh, God. "He was just embarrassed. He's very proper. Doesn't like it when people make a scene."

"Well, then you're definitely the wrong girl for him," Cynthia said with a chuckle.

Enough of that. "Back to the fashion show," DeeDee said. "Before they kick me out of here."

Cynthia handed her a notebook with lists of the tasks involved, what had been completed, and what still needed to be done.

"The town hall is booked, furniture rented, flowers and decorations ordered. Only a few things left to arrange. The biggest job will be running the event itself. You're a lifesaver, DeeDee. You're going to do a great job. I know it."

Cynthia's enthusiasm was contagious, and DeeDee found herself catching it. She could do this. She'd only participated in a few events like this and had never organized one herself, but this was her world, her wheelhouse, her comfort zone. She had this.

"I will handle this better than anything I've ever handled in my life," she promised. "It's going to be perfect."

Cynthia laughed softly. "It doesn't have to be perfect, DeeDee. I want people to have fun and learn enough about the project to open their wallets."

There was nothing she could do to help Cynthia cope with the loss of one baby, and her fear for the other, but this would at least take one burden off her plate.

"I may have to do some of the legwork with Mark in tow," DeeDee said. "Hopefully, Isaac will understand."

"I forgot to tell you. See those flowers in the corner?" Cynthia pointed to an enormous bouquet sitting on the table next to the window. "They were waiting for me when I got admitted to this room. They're from him."

DeeDee went to the window and examined the card that was sticking out of the arrangement. "Best wishes for a speedy recovery," she read. "From Isaac and Mark Litton."

He must have ordered them the second she'd left the house. Maybe he'd delivered them to the hospital himself.

"How thoughtful of him."

"Yes. Very. Especially since I've met him only the once." A slight, knowing smile touched Cynthia's lips. "I suspect this has more to do with you. Maybe he thinks you're 'okay' too."

"Whatever. I should go." DeeDee bent to brush a kiss across Cynthia's forehead. "You lie back and gestate. Don't worry about anything."

"You're taking a huge weight off my mind, DeeDee. Thank you." Cynthia pressed the button to lower the head of her bed. "I knew I could count on you."

DeeDee drove back to Maddie's place, feeling a strange mix of terror and hope. Cynthia had no reason to think she could count on DeeDee. But if anything could make up for how DeeDee had let Cynthia down in the past, this could be it.

All she had to do was pull it off.

IN THE HOSPITAL parking lot, before DeeDee started the car, before she could chicken out or forget or convince herself that it was too late to call, she picked up her cell phone and keyed in the number from Cynthia's notebook for Maya's Models.

She hated eating crow. But she'd earned this meal. She'd

do it. For Cynthia.

DeeDee pressed the button and waited. She hoped calling after business hours wouldn't annoy the woman.

"Maya Gallagher. How may I help you?"

"Maya. It's Deirdre Cash. I don't know if you remember me—"

"DeeDee! Of course I remember you. I've been following your career. I'd love to buy you a coffee sometime and hear about it. Are you back for good, or just a break?"

Whatever she'd been expecting, it wasn't this. Maya sounded friendly, her interest genuine. But if she'd really been following DeeDee's career, then she knew exactly how badly things had gone.

"Uh, my plans aren't... I don't have... I mean..." DeeDee gave a nervous bark of laughter. "My agent and I are currently on a break, so it's safe to say I'm here for the foreseeable future."

She had no idea why that had spilled out.

"I'm sorry. I didn't mean to pry," Maya said. "That's rough, but by no means insurmountable. If there's anything I can do, please ask."

DeeDee tilted her head. "Maya, that's very generous of you. I wasn't... polite to you. You know. Before."

Maya was quiet on the other end of the line.

DeeDee straightened her shoulders and swallowed hard, feeling the weight of her mistakes. She didn't deserve Maya's understanding, much less her forgiveness.

"Like I said, I've been following your career," Maya repeated. "You were young and… well. We've all been there."

"You never ended up on Tool Barn flyers," DeeDee burst out. "Or the Corn and Callus Palace. Maya, I'm sorry I was such a snot to you. And I do need to ask a favor of you. It's about Cynthia. I know you told her you don't have anyone available for her show, but please, is there anything you can do to help? She's… she's in the hospital. She was pregnant with twins, and she just lost one of them. I promised I'd fix this, and I'm begging you to help us out."

"Poor Cynthia, that's awful. But I truly have no one available. I've got plans myself that weekend, though I'll stop in if I can. I'm so sorry. Give my best to Cynthia and if I think of anything, I'll let you know immediately, okay?"

That was that. No models. DeeDee had tried, and while her heart was lighter for having apologized to Maya—for behavior she'd tried to forget—she hadn't solved Cynthia's problem.

She returned to Maddie's apartment, hugged Clementine, poured herself a glass of wine, and curled up on the floor in the spare room.

Her phone buzzed.

Isaac: *How's your sister?*

DeeDee hesitated. She hadn't expected him to ask. Was he just being polite, or did he really want to know?

DeeDee: *OK, I think. She was carrying twins. Lost one. V* *sad. Baby2 OK, but they're watching closely. Lots of monitors, etc. Xing fingers.*

No response. TMI? Probably. She'd made him uncomfortable now. Oh well. Too bad. It was nice of him to check up.

DeeDee: *Thx 4 asking. Thx 4 the flowers, 2. That was very nice of u. She appreciates it. Sorry I left u in the lurch. C u tomorrow.*

She tossed her phone aside and sipped her wine, wishing Maddie was home. But she, Chad, and their mom had insisted on taking shifts throughout the night, and Maddie wouldn't be home until two am.

It had been hard, watching Mom with Cynthia. Loss had sharpened their mom's reactions to crisis, making her brittle with fear. Apparently, Maddie was right; Mom had been more shaken up by Norm's heart attack than DeeDee realized.

More guilt. She hugged her knees and rested her head on her arms. She wanted to get into Maddie's car and drive, just drive, until all of this went away.

Her phone buzzed again, making her jump.

Isaac: *Spend tomorrow with your family. Take the week, if you want. I've made alternative arrangements for Mark. Don't worry about us. He'll miss you, but he'll be fine.*

Oh. She hadn't expected that.

The tears DeeDee had managed to control at the hospital got away from her now. She didn't know why Isaac's kindness touched her so much. Offering time off was just decent, wasn't it? And everyone sent flowers. Cynthia's room would look like a freaking hothouse nursery within a matter of days.

Isaac was a decent guy, behaving decently.

And not just to Cynthia.

To her.

DeeDee: *U sure?*

Isaac: *Yes. Let me know if there's anything I can do to help.*

The tears flowed faster. She didn't want Isaac to be a great guy. Didn't want to like him. She definitely didn't want him to like her.

DeeDee: *Thank you. I'll let u know how it goes.*

Isaac: *Hug your sister for me. Unless that's weird. Then take it for yourself.*

DeeDee laughed through her tears. She imagined Isaac's arms around her, remembering his solidness, how those lean, hard muscles had caught her when she'd fallen against him.

DeeDee: *It's a little weird. I could use a hug rt now so I'll be selfish and keep it. Thx.*

Isaac: *Selfish. Ha. Get some sleep.*

She texted him a yawning face and set her phone aside. It

was nice, having him to talk to.

Isaac was a friend, she realized with wonderment. It was tempting to think of taking things further. After all, he was hot, she was hot, proximity, opportunity—she'd never needed anything more.

But she suspected Isaac wasn't the kind of guy who had flings. Eventually, he'd find out that she was all wrapping and no gift and that, she couldn't bear.

Better to keep things friendly and avoid disappointment.

She pushed Isaac from her mind, tossed Cynthia's notebook onto the desk, crawled into bed, and pulled the covers over her head. Where else could she find models on such short notice?

DeeDee drifted off to sleep in the wee hours, only to be awakened by a dream in which Mark was shambling down a spot-lit runway, wearing his ratty khakis, the mustard-stained T-shirt, and a ball cap.

A river of chocolate ran alongside the white-draped runway. Mark squatted down, dipped his finger in, and licked it off.

"Just one," he called to DeeDee.

Mrs. Hatcher stood at the sidelines, her arms crossed. Sage cheered beside him, along with Cynthia, who carried a tightly swaddled Yorkshire terrier puppy in her arms, and Chad, who was on horseback. Mark ran back and forth. Suddenly, he was flying, and Abe and Paulie were flying with him, and everyone was laughing and there, at the end, stood

Isaac, looking at her, his grin brighter than the spotlight.

Then the night sky gave way to the light of dawn peeking around the bedroom drapes.

DeeDee blinked and rubbed her eyes. She sat up.

She had it.

This was what would save Cynthia's show. She turned on the bedside light, grabbed for a notebook and pen, and began scribbling madly.

Chapter Twelve

B Y THE TIME DeeDee had her idea fleshed out the next morning, Cynthia had been discharged. The bleeding had stopped, she wasn't having contractions, and the baby's heartbeat was strong.

What a relief! DeeDee raced out to Anders Run to meet with Cynthia, grateful that Isaac had given her the time off.

She was still warm from the smile she'd seen on his face in her dream and couldn't wait to tell him what she was planning. He'd love it. Mark would love it. It would be perfect, for everyone.

DeeDee held tightly to the steering wheel of Maddie's car as it rumbled over the bridge on the road to the Anders brothers' ranch.

She was no dummy. She knew that being without a father figure for most of her childhood had left both her and Maddie with issues around male approval. Their dating history could be summed up as quantity, not quality, and a good time, not a long time.

Until Maddie met Mick, of course.

DeeDee wasn't jealous. She was happy for Maddie. She was. Mick seemed like a great guy and with the amount of time Maddie spent out at his cabin, it appeared their relationship was heading toward permanence.

Imagine that. Her twin, heading toward marriage. Maybe even kids, one day.

DeeDee had never played with baby dolls, never doodled some boy's last name next to hers, never sought happily ever after. Happy right now, that had been her only goal.

Clothes and hair and makeup had been her girly-girl outlet, not smoochy crushes.

And now, there was Isaac.

Isaac and his smile and his flowers.

She was supposed to be focused on Mark... but it was Isaac that filled her thoughts.

Isaac. Her friend.

Her employer.

When she reached Anders Run, DeeDee found Cynthia sitting in a recliner beside the window, a soft fluffy afghan, and an even softer, fluffier cat, on her lap.

"We're all excited to hear what you've come up with, DeeDee," Cynthia said. "Even Frohike. Look at him, purring like a lawn mower."

DeeDee shook her finger. "You are not allowed to get excited. You may listen with mild interest. You may even participate in the conversation, but I expect you to sound like a slightly stoned yoga instructor high on almond milk.

You got that?"

Cynthia smiled and let her eyes go dreamy. "Ten-four, sister. I'm digging it. Chad's in the shower. He'll be right out. Eric and Logan are just outside."

"Good." DeeDee put her notebook on the gorgeous, custom-built dining room table. Chad's house had improved a great deal since she'd last seen it. It had been barely habitable then, an ancient, unloved farmhouse that was part of the property he and Eric had inherited from a grandfather they'd never met.

"Hey, DeeDee." Eric came into the room and kissed her cheek. A moment later, Logan Stafford did the same.

Logan had broken a lot of ground when he put troubled, underachieving high school students to work restoring derelict heritage houses. Marrying Samara and adopting her daughter Jade, who was on the Autism spectrum, had only furthered his passion for working with people with special needs.

DeeDee glanced at her watch. "Tell Chad to quit primping. He's pretty enough already."

"Right here." Chad emerged from the master bedroom down the hall, his hair wet from the shower, still wiping his hands on a towel. He bent over Cynthia and gave her a nuzzle. "How are you feeling, honey?"

"I'm fine, the baby's fine, we're all fine. For the ten millionth time. I'm sitting here on my butt, not doing anything." Cynthia touched his chin, and DeeDee looked away from the intimacy of the moment. She was glad her sister had found happiness. Cyn deserved it. She was truly the best person DeeDee had ever known.

"I'm also bored." Cynthia pouted. "I'm going to miss so much, stuck in the house here. I feel like such a diva."

"Just how I want you," Chad said.

"You say diva like it's a bad thing," DeeDee said. "Anyway, about the models."

"Wait. There's tea and treats in the kitchen," Cynthia said. "Chad, can you bring them out?"

Copper Mountain Chocolates, naturally. Good. That worked right into her plan.

"Did M-Maya come through?" Cynthia asked.

DeeDee took a deep breath. "No. She feels badly about it, but it is what it is."

"We're s-s-screwed." Cynthia stroked her cat and blinked hard.

"Go to your happy place, Cyn." DeeDee held out her hand. "I've already figured it out."

"I hope so." Chad's voice warned that he'd do whatever was necessary to protect his woman.

"Here's my plan." She sucked in a breath. "I'd like to use ordinary people as models. The people of Marietta. Men, women, kids, teens, seniors. And because this is a project to benefit people with special needs, why not include them as our models? You know Mark Litton, the Down syndrome guy I work with?" She glanced at the guys. "He's a great sport, and I think he'd love it. He's got a couple of friends that would probably join him."

"Friends?" Logan asked.

DeeDee shrugged. "People he works with at the May Bell Care Home."

Logan exchanged a glance with Eric and Chad.

"What? Mark's in the day program there a few hours a week." DeeDee rolled her eyes. "The woman who runs it is a little head-master-ish for me, but Isaac says it provides him with social and vocational enrichment." She put air quotes around the words.

"I'm sure Isaac wants the best for his brother." Logan chose his words carefully. "Sheltered workshops aren't known for prioritizing individual needs."

"Or even acknowledging them," Eric agreed. "Which is why we're hoping to provide an alternative. Who else do you think would participate, DeeDee?"

Isaac kept hoping Mark would adjust. But what if it wasn't Mark who needed to adjust?

"I bet Rosie Linn could get Brant and his sister Sara Maria to join in, too." She glanced at Logan. "Jade would be perfect, if you and Samara agree."

Logan pursed his lips. "Could she bring Bob?"

Jade went nowhere without her service dog, a retriever-cross she'd named Bob, despite the dog being female.

"Why not? Variety is the spice, and all that. Modeling shouldn't be restricted to…" She glanced down at herself, then shrugged. "People like me. Everyone should have a chance in the spotlight."

She forced herself to stop talking and let them think. Clenching her jaw shut, she listened to her pulse beat double time to the tick of the clock on the mantel. Patience, so not her strong suit.

"I like it," Logan said eventually. "I'll let my students know."

"Whew!" DeeDee's breath rushed out with a whoosh. "That's one. Eric?"

Eric nodded. "I like the message of inclusivity. It fits our brand."

"Chad?"

"I agree. Honey?" Chad glanced at Cynthia, awaiting her response.

"DeeDee." Cynthia's eyes shimmered and her lip wobbled. "You are the most brilliant, beautiful, fabulous sister a girl could ever ask for. Come. I want to kiss, you but I'm too high on almond milk and human bliss."

DeeDee buzzed a little, herself.

"Don't worry, Chad," she said, going to her sister. "She's only high on human chorionic gonadotropin."

Logan held his hands out sideways and looked at his friends in confusion. "Is this the same woman you used to call Ditzy DeeDee?"

"Yup," Chad said. "All grown up, planning benefits, and throwing eight-dollar words around to impress us dumb cowboys."

"Your words, not mine." DeeDee kissed the top of Cynthia's head. When Frohike head-butted her hand, she stroked the cat's silky fur. "My life works best when no one expects anything of me. This way, I get to surprise you."

"Mission accomplished," Chad said.

"And that's not all." DeeDee pointed to the plate of delicacies, remembering the river of chocolate in her dream. "I think I know how to talk Sage into donating."

"Really?" The cat, having had enough excitement, jumped off Cynthia's lap. "How?"

DeeDee shrugged one shoulder and got to her feet. "I'll tell you once I've sealed the deal."

ISAAC CONSIDERED TAKING Mark to the care home for an additional day. Without Deirdre to occupy him, Mark needed something to do and someone to be with.

"DeeDee not coming today?" Mark asked him at breakfast, his brow furrowed. "Why?"

Isaac lifted the milk jug over Mark's bowl to even out the cereal-to-milk ratio. "Her sister needs her."

"I need her." Mark hunched over his bowl, the spoon clutched in his fist like a weapon. "I don't wanna go to work."

Isaac sighed. There went that option.

He sipped his coffee, chastising himself for a coward.

The whole point of moving to Montana and downsizing his practice was so he could have the freedom to spend more time with his brother. This was the perfect opportunity to take advantage of that freedom.

"You don't have to go to your program, Mark," he said. "How about we play hooky and do something fun together today?"

Mark's head lifted fractionally, his glower unchanged. "What's hooky?"

"I don't go to work, you don't go to work, we do what we want. What do you say?"

His head came up at that. "No work for Isaac?"

His tone was full of disbelief. Isaac deserved that.

"I know, I know. I work too much." It was a familiar refrain.

But it was his income, his success, that allowed him to take responsibility for Mark, to enrich his life by moving to a house in a small town where they could relax, make friends, and breathe fresh outdoor air. Maybe even get a dog one day. He had the means to hire a companion, to take Mark to the doctors, activities, and therapy Mark needed to thrive.

Mark would always be dependent on him. Thank God he was able to provide what Mark needed.

"You work because you love me." Mark said the words he'd been told so often, the words Isaac believed but were only partially true.

Being a provider was easy. He understood that role.

Being with his brother, engaging with him, that was the challenge.

"I do love you, buddy-boy," he said, reaching out to gently punch his brother's shoulder.

A milky smile spread over Mark's face. "Can we go to Whispers and PawPaws?"

Isaac winced inwardly. He should have seen it coming. Mark and Deirdre had stopped in at the Whiskers and Paw Pals animal shelter several times since their first visit, and it was the high point of Mark's day.

"Sure, buddy," he answered. "Great idea."

Mark downed his breakfast at warp speed and was at the door, teeth brushed, hair combed, and shoes on, without a single reminder.

"Way to go, Marco." Isaac looked at the bright spring sunshine and the green buds popping out on the trees lining their street. This would be fun, he decided.

Of course, Mark's energy began flagging before they reached their destination.

"I'm hungry," he complained.

"Sorry, pal," Isaac said. "I didn't bring snacks."

DeeDee would have remembered to do that.

Mark slumped to the sidewalk. "I'm hungry and I'm tired."

"Get up." Irritation made Isaac's voice tight. "You can't sit in the middle of the street. I'll find a place to buy a snack."

ROXANNE SNOPEK

"I'm hungry and I'm tired," Mark repeated.

Isaac glanced around. A few people were going to and from cars, some young guys were jogging in the distance, and, on the other side of the street, a woman pushed a stroller, a preschooler toddling along next to her.

No one was looking at them.

What the hell.

Feeling slightly foolish, Isaac got down onto the sidewalk, facing opposite, so their backs were against each other. "Lean on me, Marco," he said. "We'll take a break and come up with a plan."

"You're my chair, and I'm your chair," Mark said.

Isaac waved to the woman with the stroller. She smiled and waved back, like it was no big deal to see two grown men sitting in the middle of the sidewalk.

A sign caught his eye.

"Gingerbread and Dessert Factory," he read. Perhaps not the best choice for a nutritious, low-fat snack, but it would certainly improve Mark's mood.

Mark looked up. "The pie store. It's the pie store!" He got to his feet awkwardly, splaying his hand on the ground to lever himself up. "It's my favorite place. I love the pie store!"

Who wouldn't? Wonderful smells emanated from the store, even from the street. The window displays reminded him of the chocolate shop Mark so loved, in that they were inviting and impossible to walk past.

Mark eagerly pushed through the doors ahead of Isaac.

"Sara Maria?" he called. "Are you here?"

What? Mark knew someone here?

"Hello, Mark." A woman came around the corner, wiping her hands on a towel. "I'm sorry, Sara Maria's not working today. But these apple turnovers are fresh from the oven, if that helps." She turned to Isaac. "Hello. I'm Rachel. You must be Mark's brother. We love it when Mark and DeeDee visit."

Isaac put out his hand. "I didn't realize they'd met so many people."

"We're a friendly town. You on your way to the shelter?" she asked Mark.

This was a regular stop? DeeDee had been feeding him baked goods and chocolate—and still somehow managed to get Mark to drop a few pounds? Impressive.

Mark nodded. "I'm hungry. I miss Sara Maria."

The woman took a pair of tongs and chose a small pastry from the tray under the counter. "I'll tell her you stopped by. Good to meet you, Isaac."

The interaction and calories boosted Mark's mood dramatically.

"So, you've got a friend named Sara Maria?" Isaac ventured.

Mark nodded vigorously. "Uh-huh. She makes pies. She smells good, like cimmanin. I like her very much. DeeDee likes her, too. DeeDee doesn't eat pie, though. Look, Isaac! There's my friend Kadoka."

Kadoka?

"Hey, Mark. Where's DeeDee?" A slender, dark-haired woman was standing behind a chain-link fence, brushing out a large dog. Or a small horse. Isaac wasn't sure which it was.

"Gone," Mark said. "Can I pet the am-i-nals?"

"Of course, you can." She gave the dog-horse a pat and stepped out of the enclosure. She wiped her hand on her jeans, and then held it out. "Hey, Isaac. We met briefly at the chocolate shop. I'm Dakota Parker. Kadoka, to Mark. Welcome to Whiskers and Paw Pet Pals. Are you looking to adopt a pet?"

He shook her hand, recalling the incident. "Not today but one day. Maybe."

Dakota grinned. "We'll see. Follow me. I'll show you where Mark and DeeDee usually start."

She led them to the cat room. Cages lined the walls, some occupied, others empty. Tall, carpet-lined climbing structures stood here and there with felines of all sizes, shapes, and colors peeking out from inside tubes, or hanging off platforms.

"Mr. Fluffy Legs!" Mark cried, moving toward a mangy-looking beast with straggly grey fur. "You're still here!"

"You bet he is, Mark." Dakota turned to Isaac. "Mr. Fluffy Legs is what we call a Lonely Heart. He's been here a long time, waiting for his forever home."

"No kidding," Isaac said. "He's not contagious, is he?"

Mr. Last Legs would be more appropriate, from what he

could see.

"He's perfectly healthy," Dakota said with a laugh. "He's had a rough life, that's all. He's picky about who he lets touch him. But he and Mark have a special bond. I'm glad you're here to see it."

The cat arched his back, yawned, then pressed his body against Mark's face as the boy gathered him in his arms.

Isaac was relieved when he put the cat down.

"Now we scoop the poop," he informed Isaac.

"Really? You and DeeDee do this?" He had a hard time picturing that.

"They're a huge help." Dakota handed Mark a pair of gloves. "It takes an army of volunteers, stopping in for an hour or two at a time, to run this place. Every little bit helps."

Isaac donned gloves and helped Mark with the tasks. It was nice to see his brother being the teacher, for once. The activity, both mental and physical, was good for him. But contributing and participating in a cause brought a glow of pride to Mark's face that warmed Isaac's heart.

How insightful of DeeDee to bring him here.

After the cats, they visited the dogs. Mark let them jump all over him, giggling and howling like one of the pack. No wonder his clothes were looking a little worse for wear. Good thing DeeDee had purchased sturdy replacements.

"Thank you," he said to Dakota when Mark showed signs of flagging again. "One day when we're ready for a pet, we'll definitely be back."

A puppy, something smart, responsive, quiet, and clean. That's what they'd get.

"Anytime," she said. "Mark, I'll see you and DeeDee soon, right?"

"Right." Mark waved in the direction of the cat room. "Bye, Mr. Fluffy Legs!"

Not a flea-bitten barn cat with trust issues.

Chapter Thirteen

TWO DAYS LATER, DeeDee forced herself to leave the ranch and head back to work with Mark. Cynthia was following doctor's orders to the letter and insisted that between Chad, Mom, and Norm, she had all the tender loving care she could handle.

DeeDee knew that saving the show would help Cynthia more than her useless hovering. She could implement her plan around Mark's schedule, anyway. But still, she felt torn.

"It's good to see you again." Isaac paused in the doorway of his office. "How's your sister?"

The concern shining in his dark eyes cracked open a tightness in her chest that she preferred to keep closed.

"Scared, I think. But still pregnant."

She remembered how Cynthia and Chad had held each other, their shoulders shaking. That was what happened when people cared. They got hurt. She swallowed, not wanting Isaac to see her distress.

"I'm so sorry. It's a loss for you, too." Isaac sounded genuine. Looked it too, his dark eyes soft with concern.

"How are you doing?"

"Me? Fine. Great." It wasn't her baby who had died, after all. "You must have dialed the florist the second you got back in the house. That was nice of you to send the flowers. She appreciated it. But you didn't have to do it. You barely know her."

His brow wrinkled. "I did it because I wanted to. It's kind of a social convention. No big deal."

"Of course." She pushed past him and hung her jacket on the coat hook. "Don't worry, I won't let this interfere with my attention to Mark. Has he had his breakfast?"

"Not yet. Deirdre, are you sure you're okay?"

She didn't know why she was picking a fight with him. "It's just… you were annoyed with me when I left early to go see her. You were busy, you had a ton of stuff on your mind, and you were inconvenienced. And then you sent me those texts. They were… very nice."

"I owed you that much." He met her gaze calmly. "My initial reaction was selfish and thoughtless. As soon as I realized it, I corrected my action. Nothing's more important than family. Of course I'll support you in being there for yours. Did it bother her to receive flowers from her sister's employer?"

"No, of course not. They're beautiful. But she wondered…"

His eyebrows lifted. "Yes?"

She decided to be blunt. "Cynthia wondered if you sent

the flowers because of me."

A slight smile tickled his lips. "What if I did?"

She wasn't expecting that. "What does that mean?"

"It means," Isaac said slowly, "that you are kind to my brother, so naturally, I want to be kind to your sister in return."

"Oh." Nothing more than reciprocity, then. "In that case, thank you. Again. Very thoughtful of you."

"I'm glad you think so. I appreciate everything you're doing for Mark, Deirdre. And for me. I went to the shelter with him yesterday. He loves it there."

"He loves Mr. Fluffy Legs." She grimaced. "Don't ask me how that happened. But I think there's a very ugly cat in your future."

"Not if I can help it." He thumped the heel of his hand to his forehead. "That's the sorriest creature I've ever seen."

"Might be why Mark loves him."

"He certainly recognizes the outcasts. But seriously, I'm grateful for how you've introduced him to new people and places. It's done wonders for his self-esteem." He paused. "I think he's met more people in Marietta than I have."

Was that loneliness in his voice?

"You should come with us on our walks," she said. "You can't help but meet people that way."

He looked away. "Maybe. Thanks. Listen, Deirdre, I hope you know that if you need anything from me, all you have to do is ask."

There it was again, that little burst of joy she didn't know what to do with. Where was the line between doing things for others and getting trapped in a lifetime of obligation?

It was so much easier to be selfish.

So much safer.

"On that note," she said, moving away from uncomfortable emotional territory, "I need to hit up a couple of local businesses for donations. Is it okay if I combine it with Mark's walk?"

Isaac's expression clouded. "He might make things difficult for you."

"One of our stops will be Copper Mountain Chocolates, so I don't think he'll mind. Since this project is to benefit that alternative program Cynthia told you about for people with special needs, I think having Mark along would be a bonus."

Isaac crossed his arms. "You want to use my brother as a prop for charity?"

DeeDee crossed her own arms. "Weren't we just talking about how great it is that he's meeting new people?"

"Under certain circumstances, yes. But if you've got business to attend to, he might get bored or frustrated. That won't do either of you any good."

"He's pretty decent company and not as prone to embarrassing displays as you seem to think."

Isaac's lips tightened. He looked away. "Easy to say when

you haven't seen one."

DeeDee rolled her eyes. "Whatever. He can stay here and watch TV, if that's what you'd prefer. You're the boss."

Biting back her irritation, she went upstairs to prepare Mark's oatmeal. She and Isaac had been having a moment, and then he had to go all negative on her.

After being so nice, too.

She couldn't figure him out.

So, she focused on Mark, instead. Simple, straightforward, affectionate Mark. No wonder people loved him.

They spent the next few hours unpacking the vast supply of dry and canned goods that had been tossed into boxes regardless of best-before dates.

"You, Marco, eat entirely too much processed foods," she told him.

"This is my favorite of all." He held up a box of microwaveable macaroni and cheese.

"That's not food. It's packaging material."

At noon, she and Mark walked to the grocery store for vegetables and fruit. She made a game of arranging apple slices, almonds, cheddar cheese, and whole-grain crackers onto a tray for their lunch. Then, on a whim, she made up a third plate.

"Let's take your brother a snack, shall we?"

Mark complied eagerly, carrying the plate downstairs in a careful walk. DeeDee pushed the office door open and peeked inside so as not to disturb Isaac.

He had his headset on and was deep in conversation via Skype. On a second monitor, he adjusted an Excel spreadsheet.

His hair was rumpled from the device and the tails of his white dress shirt had come free from the waistband of his jeans, but the crisp collar portrayed just the right amount of casual professionalism. He was in his element, deaf and blind to anything else around him.

DeeDee motioned for Mark to set the plate on the side table, and they backed out without a word.

After lunch, cleanup, tooth brushing, and a rest, she glanced outside. The afternoon sunshine could not have been more inviting.

"Ready for our walk?" she asked. She should never have mentioned to Isaac that they were going to make a few extra stops. This would be no different from the shelter, the bakery, the park, or the coffee shop.

"I'm tired," he replied. "I wanna watch TV."

She'd anticipated that. "I've got treats planned for you."

His bottom lip pouched out, but she knew she'd snagged his attention. "What treats?"

"Something for now and something for later. Let's put our shoes on, and then we'll have the first treat. The second one is a surprise." Given how much he liked Sage's shop, it was a safe bet that her chocolate would be a powerful motivator.

As they put their shoes on, the door to Isaac's office

opened. "You guys heading out?"

"Places to go, people to see. Unless you still have objections?"

He didn't respond.

Good. In her book, that meant approval. She pressed a tall plastic container into Mark's hand. "Here's your first treat."

Mark looked doubtfully at the container. "What's that?"

"It's a smoothie. You'll love it. It's like a milkshake but better."

It was a *kale* smoothie, but Mark didn't need to know specifics.

"Why is it so green?"

"Because it's special, just like you and me." She took a long pull on the straw of her own container. "Delicious. I love being special. Don't you?"

Mark took a hesitant sip, thought a moment, then took another. "Isaac's special, too. Doesn't he get one?"

DeeDee looked at Isaac. "I don't know. Are you special, Isaac?"

Isaac took off his sexy glasses and rubbed his eyes. Then he blew out a breath and a tired smile broke over his face. "Sure, why not?" In a low smoky voice, he added, "Thanks for the fruit platter. You may have saved my life."

Again, heat warmed her chest, pushing the irritation away. "That's me, superhero with a paring knife. We'll be back in an hour. Don't worry about a thing, okay? We'll be fine." On a whim, she decided to try again. "You're still welcome to join us, of course."

Isaac frowned, glanced over his shoulder, then seemed to come to a decision. "Give me a minute to get changed."

"Yes," Mark said, clapping his hands. "Come with us, Isaac! You can share my smoothie!"

"Awesome." DeeDee gave him a questioning glance. "You sure you have the time?"

His lip quirked up. "I've got the same amount as everyone else. Luckily, as someone recently reminded me, I'm the boss." He took a step closer. "I get to choose my priorities. Right now, I choose to spend that time with someone who's important to me."

Mark. He meant Mark.

So why was he looking at her like that?

ISAAC KEPT A close eye on his brother as they made their way through the park, toward the downtown area. Dotted among the storefronts were terra-cotta pots filled with brilliant yellow-flowering shrubs, beneath which cheery snowdrops, crocuses, and early tulips proclaimed an end to the wintery weather. Mark chattered steadily to DeeDee, who stopped patiently with him to admire the blossoms or to greet a passerby.

Mark kept up easily, his fitness already improved by the daily walks. Focusing on his brother helped him not focus on

DeeDee, though given her cheerful energy, that wasn't easy. Every time she laughed, batted that thick ponytail off her shoulder, or bent to smell a flower, he found himself unable to look away.

He forced his attention back to Mark. Recently, he'd noticed a subtle change in Mark's demeanor. He seemed perkier, more engaged. Isaac cast his eye over the red-and-white T-shirt with long sleeves and the dark-wash jeans DeeDee had bought for him. Between the clothes, the hair, and the trendy high-top sneakers, all Mark needed was a skateboard to fit in with half the young men in the park.

Points to DeeDee on that.

Still, too much change and stimulation could easily overwhelm Mark, especially in the witching hours of late afternoon. When they reached the storefront of Two Old Goats wine store, Isaac reached for his brother's arm.

"We'll stay out here. Okay, buddy? DeeDee needs to go inside to talk to the owners."

Mark's face fell. "I wanna go in."

There was so much glass inside.

"Don't be silly, Isaac." DeeDee opened the door. "Come on in, both of you."

She introduced herself, Isaac, and Mark to the proprietors, Clifford Yerks and Emerson Moore, a couple of retired wine aficionados living out their dream. The men shook hands with each of them, then listened avidly as DeeDee pitched her proposal with skill and polish.

As she ran through the details, Isaac realized he hadn't appreciated the potential of this project. He'd been too distracted and embarrassed that day in the chocolate shop to do more than write Cynthia a check.

Embarrassed by the scene Mark had caused.

Distracted by DeeDee's pretty bra.

"A fashion show for a special needs support program," Clifford said. "We'd be happy to contribute."

He had an easy smile and the comfortable physique of a man who enjoyed his food without apology.

"Any excuse to show off our wine." Emerson, the leaner of the two, but just as friendly, began pulling out several bottles. "We'll need to taste a few to make sure you get the right one."

Mark watched closely. "Yay! Can I taste, too?"

Isaac's instant reaction was to say no. To his knowledge, his brother had never been exposed to alcohol and with him already tired and hungry, Isaac couldn't see this going well. He opened his mouth to explain that Mark wouldn't care for it, but DeeDee stilled him with a hand to his arm.

"Are you over twenty-one?" Clifford asked.

Mark nodded vigorously. "I'm twenty-four."

"Then of course you can." Emerson pulled out an elegantly labeled bottle and poured a splash for each of them. "This off-dry Riesling has delicious citrus notes."

Mark took one mouthful, coughed, and put his glass on the counter. "Too sour."

"Different strokes for different folks." Unfazed, Emerson lifted a bottle of fizzy-flavored water. "Would you like to try this instead?"

The sweet beverage more to his liking, Mark sipped and swirled along with the rest of them, and Isaac began to relax. He'd never have imagined himself sharing such an ordinary pleasure with his brother.

The convivial atmosphere and easy acceptance of Mark gave Isaac a buzz that had nothing to do with the tiny samples of wine. Perhaps it was the joy of being outside in the sunshine after a season of too much time indoors.

"Thank you so much," DeeDee said, pressing their hands in turn after they'd agreed to donate several cases of sparkling white and rosé to the fashion show.

"Can't say no to a pretty face," one said. He winked at Isaac. "I'm sure you know all about that."

"Oh." Isaac looked at DeeDee. "It's not…"

"Emerson sees romance everywhere." Clifford laughed and clapped him on the back. "You do make a handsome couple though, I have to say. Nice to meet you, Mark," he added. "Looking forward to seeing you strut your stuff."

Wait. What?

The bell above the door tinkled as they exited the store. Once on the sidewalk again, DeeDee did a little skip.

"One down!" Her eyes twinkled. "Aren't they the sweet-est old guys? This'll be so great for the show."

"Cynthia will be happy," he said. "What did they mean

about Mark strutting his stuff?"

Deirdre smiled. "He's going to be one of the models. A couple of Mark's friends are participating, including the girl from the bakery. She's nice. Isn't she, Mark?"

Isaac stopped. "Did I miss a memo? Mark, a model?"

"Sara Maria," Mark said. "She makes pies. I like pies. I want to be boyfriend and girlfriend with her."

Whoa. Picturing Mark on stage was bad enough. But a girlfriend? Where had that come from?

He looked at Deirdre, who was smiling even more broadly now.

"A lot can happen in a day or two," she said airily. "I was going to tell you."

Isaac pulled out his cell phone and handed it to Mark. "Play your game for a few minutes while I talk to Deirdre. Okay, buddy?"

DEEDEE SHOULDERED OPEN the door to Copper Mountain Chocolates, hoping Sage would be as agreeable as the men from Two Old Goats had been.

And more agreeable than Isaac. His big-brother protectiveness was heartwarming—to a point. He needed to lighten up. Mark would be on stage for two minutes, tops. The attention would do him good. Same thing with his budding friendship with Sara Maria. An intellectual disability didn't preclude a crush, apparently. It was sweet.

"Remember this place?" she asked Mark.

"Yeah." Mark's eyes were wide as saucers, taking in the beautiful window displays. "Can we buy some, Isaac? Please?"

"We'll see," Isaac said. He still looked pissy about his brother wanting to be in the "close-show," as Mark referred to it.

"Remember the treat we're having after our walk?" Dee-Dee said, ignoring Isaac.

"Oh!" Mark clapped his hands. "Chocolate! My favorite."

Everything he liked was his favorite.

"I'll talk to my friend first. That okay, Markie?"

DeeDee waited to be certain Mark understood before approaching the counter.

The smell inside the shop made her mouth water. It was getting harder and harder to resist temptation.

She glanced at Isaac, catching him looking at her, his expression shuttered. Some people needed to be pushed. But had she gone too far? Then he blinked once, slowly, and the chill left his dark eyes. He tipped his head ever so slightly, as if perplexed but willing to live with the uncertainty.

Willing to trust her.

Something soft and warm fizzed inside her. Like the homely cat at the shelter, Isaac didn't trust easily.

"Welcome to Copper Mountain Chocolates."

A young woman DeeDee didn't recognize looked up

from where she was stirring the copper pot filled with Sage's decadent hot cocoa. The Carrigan family resemblance, plus the mound beneath the woman's apron, made DeeDee guess this was the niece Cynthia had mentioned, the one who'd quit college to work for Sage while she waited for her baby to be born.

The one for whom Sage had been trying to plan a baby shower for. The shower Cynthia was going to help with before the miscarriage derailed everything.

"You're just in time to sample a fresh batch of champagne truffles."

DeeDee smiled. The girl was young enough that they'd have missed each other entirely in high school. "I wish. I don't know how you work here and manage to stay so skinny. You must be Portia."

"I am." Portia blushed, glancing down at her baby bump. "You call this skinny?"

"You've got good lines, nice bone structure. I bet once Junior is out, you'll be back to rocking it. I'm DeeDee. Is your boss here?"

"Aunt Sage is in the back," Portia said. "Should I know you?"

DeeDee didn't know whether to be relieved or sad that the young woman had no idea who she was. "I grew up here, but I've been gone for a while. You probably know my sister, Maddie."

"Maddie Cash." Instantly, Portia's demeanor softened.

"Of course. You're her twin. I'm a twin, too. Nice to finally meet you. I've heard a lot about you. You're even prettier than everyone says."

DeeDee's face warmed. She doubted that was all people said about her. But it was nice of Portia to be polite.

"I wanted to talk to your aunt about a fundraiser I think she'll want to be involved in."

"That's great," Portia said. "We're trying to get Sage to market her products properly, but she's the worst self-promoter. Let me get her for you. While you're waiting, why don't you try the truffles?"

"I'm sure my friend Mark will be happy to try them," DeeDee said with a smile.

Portia lifted a sample with the tongs and dropped it into Mark's hand. "You'll love this."

"One piece only, please," Isaac said, watching Mark carefully.

They took their samples and sat down at one of the small tables to wait for her. Mark's cheeks puckered inward as he savored his treat, an expression of bliss on his face.

DeeDee leaned against the counter, tapping her toes on the tile floor. She eyed the small sample plate of cut-up truffles. They were very small. Perhaps just one.

She was reaching for the smallest piece she could find when Sage pushed through the door backward, a tray of fresh product balanced on her shoulder.

DeeDee jumped back, dropped the piece of candy, and

managed to knock the whole plate onto the floor, sending bits of champagne truffle across the pristine floor.

"You made a messy-mess," Mark said.

"I did." DeeDee gave Sage an apologetic grin. "Sorry. But you saved me from myself. Got a broom?"

Sage wore a lovely pale shade of lipstick that complimented her fair complexion and red-gold hair. The entire shop seemed designed to complement her coloring. She was in her element, a pearl glowing against a black velvet backdrop.

How lovely to have found your place in the world so perfectly, DeeDee thought.

"What is it with you and Maddie and my chocolate?" Sage set the tray on the glass topped display case and slid open the door. "She went almost an entire month without eating her very favorite chocolate-covered Himalayan salted caramels, thanks to a ridiculous New Year's resolution. If you've given up chocolate for Lent, I do not want to hear about it."

Was she imagining the faint note of animosity? Sage had been friendly earlier when she'd been here with Cynthia.

But everyone knew that Me-Me-DeeDee had been less than supportive of Cynthia in the past. Cynthia, whom everyone loved, and for good reason.

Then again, there were dark smudges beneath Sage's eyes that suggested she hadn't slept long enough recently. Easter was, as Cynthia said, a busy time for a chocolatier.

"Sage, you remember Mark Litton, your biggest fan, and his brother, Isaac." She turned to Isaac. "You and Mark can wait for me outside, if you want."

Isaac sat back in the chair and stretched out his legs. "We're good."

"I like it here, DeeDee," Mark said. "It's my favorite place."

"Mark's most impressed with the fact that you make everything here yourself," DeeDee said.

Mark gazed at Sage with adoration. "Are you magic?"

Sage laughed. "No. But it seems magical, doesn't it?"

She shoved the tray into the display case and closed the glass door. Then she took the broom and quickly swept up the mess DeeDee had made.

"How's Cynthia doing?"

DeeDee updated her. "Her latest ultrasound showed a healthy baby, so we're hoping for the best. But she's on bedrest for at least another month, so I've taken over running the fashion show."

"That's a lot for you to take on," Sage said. "I hope you can handle it. No one deserves a happy ending more than Cynthia."

Her point, DeeDee understood, was to stake her claim as Cynthia's friend and remind DeeDee that any repetitions of sisterly misconduct would not be tolerated.

She was uncomfortably aware of Isaac listening to their conversation.

"Just so you know, Sage, I'm well aware of my shortcomings." She swallowed. "I won't let her down again."

Sage busied herself setting the new delicacies in the display case. Her long braid fell over her shoulder as she bent to put away the broom and dustpan. When she finished, she straightened up, looked at DeeDee another minute, then sighed.

"Sorry. I'm tired and cranky. I shouldn't have put that on you. What can I get you?"

DeeDee heaved a sigh of relief. "A dozen champagne truffles, ten minutes of your time, and an open mind."

"I'm intrigued." She went to the case containing the special truffles. With a pair of tongs, she took out twelve and placed them in one of her signature copper-colored boxes.

The dark chocolate surface of the truffles glistened, each one with a tiny flourish on top, unique but uniform, handmade and as exquisite to look at as they tasted.

DeeDee paid for her purchase and handed the package to Isaac. "Why don't you guys wait for me outside? I won't be long."

Isaac turned his face and lowered his voice. "Ex-nay on the awclat-chay. He's already had plenty."

"Is that my 'prise, DeeDee?" Mark bounced in his chair.

"One piece," she said firmly. "Surely you can live with that, Isaac."

Considering the improvements she'd already made to Mark's diet, Isaac was being ridiculous. Mark was far more flexible than big brother gave him credit for.

"Now," Sage said, leading her to a table. "What did you want to talk about?"

"Cynthia won't ask, so I'm asking for her. You know about the fundraiser fashion show she's organizing for Building Tomorrow. We need some elegant nibble for the tables. Clifford and Emerson are donating sparkling wine, but we need something more. Copper Mountain Chocolates would be perfect. It's a great opportunity to further your brand and support a good cause at the same time."

"You sound like Krista, my marketing guru." Sage sighed. "All I want to do is make chocolate and bring joy to my customers. But everyone else wants me to go to the next level. I can barely keep up with this level. I wish I could, DeeDee, but between eggs, bunnies, special orders, gift baskets, and spring displays, all I can think about is grabbing a few hours of sleep. When the kids let me. I promised Dawson that as soon as Easter's done, I'm taking a break." Her face fell. She glanced toward the counter and lowered her voice. "And I still have a certain important event to organize."

"I'm offering a trade." DeeDee also glanced at Portia, who was busy with a couple of tourists. She leaned closer to Sage. "You contribute chocolate for the tables. And I'll handle the... special event."

Sage cupped one hand around her mouth and whispered, "You are talking about Portia's baby shower, right? I meant to ask Cynthia but, obviously, that's out of the question now. You'd do that?"

"I'm good at parties, remember?" She gave Sage a wry look.

"This is an important one." Sage's shoulders drooped. "I wish she'd tell me what's going on. Keeping secrets is hard. I almost spilled the beans myself yesterday about a customer who sent chocolates to our 'least likely to get a Valentine' Marietta resident." Instantly, she squeezed her eyes shut. "Pretend you didn't hear that."

"No way." Seeing the normally composed Sage flustered warmed DeeDee's heart. "Carol Bingley? Mrs. Hatcher?" Then she gasped. "His Honor the crab! That's it, isn't it?"

Someone sent chocolates to miserable, reclusive Judge Kingsley? Just walking past his neglected mansion sent shivers up her spine.

"You didn't hear that from me." Sage made a lock-and-key motion at her lips. "And his mystery admirer stays in the vault. But see what I mean? Secrets are awful. We need to show you-know-who that we love and support her, no matter what her situation. No questions asked."

"I can do that, Sage. I promise. Tell me what you want."

Sage bit her lip, thinking. "The most important thing is that… the guest of honor… is celebrated like a queen. It would be awesome having someone like you running point. You'd be able to focus on the logistics instead of chatting, since you aren't really…"

Sage stopped. Her creamy complexion turned pink.

DeeDee understood perfectly. The warmth of a moment ago disappeared, but it wasn't Sage's fault. DeeDee wasn't part of the social scene here anymore, never had been, really. Friends wouldn't distract her, so she was the perfect one to do the fetching and carrying.

DeeDee pushed down the hurt and pasted on her best, camera-ready smile. It wasn't personal. She wasn't doing this for herself; she was doing this for Cynthia.

"So, do we have a deal?" she said.

Chapter Fourteen

"YOU INDULGE HIM too much." Isaac frowned as Deirdre set out a plate of what he guessed was some kind of baked good in preparation for Mark's return from his morning at the care home. The day program, he believed, still had value for Mark, especially now that Mark had other activities to look forward to as well. Variety was important. It helped develop flexibility and adaptability, qualities Mark struggled with.

DeeDee used the time to prepare those activities, and Isaac was especially impressed with her latest plan. Logan Stafford had invited her to bring Mark to Chad's woodworking shop, where they were trying out an informal drop-in program. Sharp tools and special needs didn't seem like a good combination to him, but Mark had come home from his first time there thrilled to bits.

"I'll have you know," she said, rearranging the lumps until they were just so, "that these cookies are made with whole grains, high in fiber, full of natural dried fruits, and sweetened with a touch of honey. I made them myself, so I know they're good for him. Unlike the store-bought stuff you've been giving him."

They were cookies. Could have fooled him. "You baked?"

"What did you think that smell was, air freshener? Yes, Ike, I baked."

It annoyed him to no end that she insisted on using the nickname, but he refused to let her see. It would just encourage her.

Plus, he couldn't ignore the tiny bit of warmth implied by the familiarity. People didn't speak in such a way to someone they feared or mistrusted. She'd given him a pass to the kind of special in-circle he associated with family or friends.

Which made no sense.

"Methinks the lady doth protest too much."

Deirdre rolled her eyes. "So I'm a beginner. We all start somewhere. It's not rocket science. They taste better than they look. Here. Try one."

She held a chunk up to his mouth.

She was close enough that he could see the striations in her irises. Blue, gold, little strands of green, too. Was that her natural eye color, or did she wear colored contacts?

He could smell her too. Something lighter than usual but still spicy. Underneath, there was the warm smell of shower-fresh clean skin, even this late in the day.

Instantly, the image of DeeDee standing naked under a

spray of water filled his mind. Her caramel-streaked hair running in a dark rivulet down her bare back, her arms lifted, her head thrown back, eyes closed in ecstasy as the cascade rushed over her.

"Good, huh?"

He swallowed the mouthful. It went down, so it must have been edible, but the aftertaste of vanilla was all he could identify.

"It'll do," he said.

"They're delicious and you know it." She opened the refrigerator and poured a glass of milk. "After, I've lined up a fun activity for Mark. I was hoping you'd join us."

She made the offer casually, wiping down the counter without looking at him, but he sensed that she was nervous.

"What's the activity?" He had a couple of reports to finish, but he could put them off until tomorrow.

"Something Sage suggested. Trust me, it'll be fun."

The door crashed downstairs then as Mark burst through it and ran up to greet them.

"DeeDee, DeeDee," he shouted, shoving something into her hands. "Look what I made for you. Can we go see Mr. Fluffy Legs today? And Kadoka?"

"Easy, buddy," she told him. "I'm right here. No need to yell down the walls. We'll see your cat tomorrow. We've got a different activity for today."

She dutifully admired the cardboard picture frame, which Isaac could see had been prefabbed by a hobby supply outlet. Mark had only glued the pieces together and decorated it, but he was so proud.

"Wash up for snack time," she said. "Then, I've got a surprise for you."

Few other words had the same effect on Mark. He stormed down the hallway to the bathroom, his lumbering footfalls making the light fixtures shake in their housings.

Isaac turned to the stairs. "I've got two calls to make. Let me know when you're ready to start this mysterious activity."

DeeDee's face opened like the sunrise. "Really? You'll join us? That's wonderful. I mean, Mark will be so glad."

He hadn't expected her enthusiasm.

"Mark?" he said softly. "Not you?"

Her eyes widened, then a smile teased her lips. "Do you want me to be glad?"

Heat rose lazily within him, stretched and curled. Her lips were plump and inviting. She was easy to be around, fun, funny, and wasn't bothered by Mark. In fact, she seemed to genuinely enjoy his company.

Mark. He gave his head a shake. What was he thinking, flirting with her? Deirdre was here for Mark, not him.

"I'm hungry," Mark said from behind them. "Why do those meatballs smell like cimmanin?"

SAGE HAD GIVEN DeeDee the idea, based on the Easter treat she was retooling for the fashion show, a white-chocolate bark dotted with homemade mini-eggs coated in a multitude of pastel colors.

Isaac and Mark had no family around to celebrate Easter with, which DeeDee found sad. Part of her wanted to invite them to the ranch for one of her mom's lavish family dinners.

Another part of her shuddered at the prospect. Mom would make assumptions, Maddie would say something embarrassing, Mick would clap Isaac on the back in a manly, congratulatory way despite there being nothing to congratulate him on.

Because they weren't involved.

Not like that, at least. Though they kept having moments…

What was wrong with her? Where was all this coming from? She was thinking as if she was… attracted to Isaac.

As if she… liked him.

Well, of course she liked him. She wouldn't be working for him if she didn't.

No, her brain argued. *Like* him, like him.

Which was crazy.

Almost as crazy as imagining herself in an argument with her brain.

"Easter Egg Bark," she announced, her voice bouncing loudly off the walls. She cleared her throat. "The project, I mean. Since you aren't doing anything for Easter, I thought it would be a fun way to celebrate spring. And… Easter…"

"We're going to church on Easter Sunday," Mark said.

Isaac looked like he was holding in laughter.

"Oh," DeeDee said. "That's good. Well, anyway. This is fun, super pretty, easy, and quick. And delicious." She had to rethink her caffeine ingestion. This was ridiculous. She forced herself to take a deep breath.

"First, we chop the white chocolate," DeeDee said. "Isaac, will you handle this part, please?"

She set a cutting board and a large bar of silky smooth white chocolate in front of him, trying to ignore the fact that he smelled better than any sweet treat.

"What do I do?" Mark clapped his hands. "I want to help."

"Of course," DeeDee said. "We need one scoop of mini-eggs in this bowl, a scoop of smarties in this bowl, and then you have to choose which sprinkles you want."

"I want them all," he said promptly.

"Okay," she responded with a laugh. It didn't much matter what they used.

Sage wouldn't dream of using commercially available candies for her recipes; it was what made her stuff special. DeeDee's project was more about fun and letting Mark share in the joy of Sage's creative genius.

"Good," DeeDee said. "The next step is to put the bowl of chopped chocolate into the microwave."

Isaac picked up the bowl.

"No," she said. "Let Mark do it."

"I do it," Mark said.

"Don't drop it," Isaac cautioned.

DeeDee touched his arm. "Relax, Ike. This is supposed to be fun."

Mark put the bowl into the microwave, then punched the buttons as directed.

"Don't stand so close, Mark," Isaac said. "Radiation is bad for you."

"Your attitude is bad for him," she said, exasperated. "I hate to tell you this, but no one gets out of life alive."

Isaac pressed his lips together.

The timer went off, and Mark clapped again. "It's ready?"

She checked the chocolate, gave it a stir, set it for another thirty seconds, and went to find parchment paper for the cookie sheets.

"Now?" Mark was nearly beside himself. "Now?"

"Almost. It needs another stir. It's still warming up."

The microwave dinged, then Mark reached in with both hands.

"Wait, Mark! Use oven mitts," she called, but he was already pulling the Pyrex bowl out.

"Ow-ow-ow!" he yelped, dropping it.

And holy sweet napalm, the bowl shattered, sending chunks of broken glass and semi-molten chocolate everywhere—on the stovetop, the counter, the cabinets, Mark's clothing, the floor.

"Mark! Are you okay?" Isaac skidded in a puddle of chocolate and nearly fell. "Damn it, don't move."

Mark was sobbing. "Sorry, sorry, sorry. I made a mess. Sorry. Ow, ow, ow."

DeeDee grabbed a roll of paper towels and turned the cold-water faucet on. "Did you burn your hands, honey? Let me see."

She led Mark carefully away from the broken glass and turned his palms over. No burns, just a bit of redness. He'd been surprised, that's all.

"Hold them under the cold water, okay? It'll take away the sting."

"I sorry, sorry, sorry." Mark was full-on weeping.

"Damn it," Isaac muttered again. "This is a disaster. I knew this was a bad idea."

"You're not helping, Ike," she said in a singsong voice. "How about grabbing a trash can for the shrapnel and save the recriminations for the court martial."

He gave her a dirty look but tiptoed to the closet where the cleaning supplies were kept.

"This isn't a disaster," she said in a matter-of-fact tone.

"Oh yeah?" Isaac gestured to Mark. "What do you call that?"

Mark was quaking, rocking, and muttering, snot and tears dripping off his chin.

Maybe it was a disaster. What did she know?

"Look at me, Mark," she instructed.

He ignored her, continuing to moan and rock.

"Disaster." Isaac snapped the cupboard door shut. "He'll be like this until he goes to bed, then he'll probably be up once or twice in the night, upset again. You haven't lived with him. You don't know him."

Isaac's criticism stung. But it was true. She hadn't known Mark long, and her entire education about mental disabilities had come from the reading she'd done over the past few weeks.

Isaac obviously knew better.

Isaac, Logan Stafford, Mrs. Hatcher, heck, everyone at the May Bell Care Home.

DeeDee, in her ignorance, had assumed that caring for Mark would be a simple task when, in fact, she'd barely scratched the surface of what it took to care for a person with special needs.

"I'm sorry," she said. "You're right." She turned off the faucet and pressed a dish towel into Mark's hands. She wiped his face, stroked his hair, then pulled him close.

"I sorry," Mark sobbed into her shoulder. "Sorry, sorry, sorry."

Isaac gently pried Mark away. "Let's get you cleaned up, buddy." His voice was resigned. "DeeDee, can you handle the rest of this mess?"

She swallowed, fighting her own tears. "Yes."

Cleaning up messes. She had plenty of experience there.

188

IT HAD TAKEN Isaac an hour to get Mark cleaned up and settled down enough to take a nap. Hopefully, when he woke up, he'd be in a better frame of mind, but Isaac wasn't holding his breath.

DeeDee had everything sparkling once more when he joined her in the kitchen, broken glass gone, melted chocolate wiped up. The bowls of candy remained neatly on the table, as well as a fresh container of chopped white chocolate and the prepared pans.

"You don't need to finish it, you know," he told her. "He'll probably forget all about it."

DeeDee raised her eyebrows. "But I promised him. He was so excited. It won't take long and this time, I'll make sure he uses oven mitts."

Her eyes were a clear blue-green, wide and innocent. Determined, but so naive. She meant well. She was expanding Mark's comfort zone. Mark was making friends, doing new things, and having fun, just as Isaac wanted.

But there was a limit. DeeDee didn't seem to get that.

"Best to find a new project, one better suited to his… skill level."

"This *is* his skill level. He broke a bowl. He didn't blow up the house."

"It may not seem like much to you." Isaac worked to keep his voice calm. "Emotional outbursts are hard on him. It's important to avoid anything that might set him off. You've only seen the tip of the iceberg. Sometimes, he cries so hard he throws up. He bangs his head until he gets a nosebleed. He hits himself. He throws things. That's why I don't want him participating in your show. Stress and crowds aren't his thing. He might think he wants to do it now, but on the day, he'll freak out. Neither of us wants that."

She swiped a cloth over the already-gleaming surface. There was a smear of white chocolate on the back of her shirt. The set to her jaw suggested that she disagreed with him.

But to his surprise, she didn't argue.

"I didn't know." She folded the cloth and hung it over the sink. "I apologize. Of course you know your brother best."

Isaac scrubbed a hand over the bristle on his chin, feeling like a heel. "I didn't mean to come down on you so hard."

She braced her arms on the table between them, looking down. "Don't worry, I'll get over it. I deserve it. I have a long history of not paying attention to what other people need, of leaping onto the next shiny thing, regardless of whether it's a good idea or not, or if I've left someone else in the lurch. Me-Me-DeeDee. Ditzy-DeeDee." She gave a little laugh. "I'm trying to change, but old habits, you know. If you don't want him in the show, then he won't be in the show. I should know better than to talk to him without asking you first."

Something inside Isaac's chest pinched him. He liked

that she treated Mark as she did. She listened, which was more than Isaac could say sometimes. Even though Mark didn't always know what was best for him, DeeDee gave him the same respect—or lack thereof—that she gave anyone else.

"DeeDee." He took a step toward her, coming around the side of the table and closing the gap between them.

"What?" She tossed her head as if annoyed with herself.

A silky strand of hair had come free from her ponytail, drifting over her cheek. He reached out and tucked it behind her ear. "You're good for Mark."

"Ha." Her dark lashes swept up, then down, as she glanced briefly at him.

He wasn't used to her being hesitant.

He didn't like it.

"You're good for me, too."

She looked up again. This time, she held his gaze. The delicate muscles and tendons of her neck shifted as she swallowed, and he heard the little click in her throat.

He was so close he could feel the warmth of her body, smell the hint of sweetness on her breath. She was breathing quickly, the thin white fabric of her T-shirt moving up and down, reminding him of the soft curves beneath.

"You're... something else," he whispered. He touched her chin with his bent knuckle. "Beautiful."

She inhaled sharply, closing her eyes and tilting her head sideways. "Please. I'm not even wearing makeup."

He tipped her chin toward him again. "I like you best

like this. The real you. Naturally perfect." And she was. Her skin was like satin or velvet or silk, her lips plump and inviting. He bent his head closer, lower, already tasting her in his imagination.

"Isaac?"

He leaped backward. "Mark," he said. "You're up. How are you feeling, buddy?"

Deirdre brushed the hair away from her face, a flush staining her cheeks. "Did you have a nice nap, Marco?"

Mark looked back and forth between them, then focused on the candy on the table. His eyes brightened. "Can we finish making my magic chocolate now?"

Chapter Fifteen

"HE KISSED YOU?" Maddie lifted her hand for a high-five, almost knocking over the wine bottle between them on the coffee table. "See? I knew there was something there."

Clementine jumped on Maddie's lap, ready to defend her.

"Yeah, yeah. Maddie knows best." DeeDee rolled her eyes, halfheartedly slapped her twin's hand, then chucked the little dog under the chin. "And there was no kiss. It was an incomplete pass. Mark intercepted us before we made contact."

To DeeDee's eternal regret. Her lips were still sizzling with Isaac's nearness, the warmth that had so nearly touched her. Something had combusted between her and Isaac at that moment, something that had been brewing and simmering for weeks, something she hadn't quite recognized until it snapped into sharp focus and now, she couldn't stop imagining it. Fantasizing about it. Picturing in her head.

Isaac's lips on hers. Isaac's hand on the back of her neck.

Isaac's fingers in her hair. His breath on her throat, his teeth nipping gently at her skin...

"Then we have to engineer another opportunity." Maddie tapped her fingers together. "That shouldn't be difficult."

DeeDee took a sip of wine. Her hand was shaking. "Not your business. Stay out of it."

"Look. I don't charge you rent. The least you can do is give me an outlet for my natural-born talents. Cynthia never listens to me anymore now that she's got Chad."

Maddie made a face. DeeDee knew that under the bravado, they were equally relieved that their stepsister was doing well. Their little niece or nephew was quietly and obediently incubating according to plan, and Cynthia had been upgraded to light activity. DeeDee, however, refused to let her take back any responsibilities. The show was nearly ready anyway.

"I can pay rent," she said. She'd rather do that than get her own place, as finding an apartment of her own seemed so... permanent. She hadn't thought that far yet.

Though what she was waiting for, she couldn't say.

"Have you talked to him since then?" Maddie asked.

DeeDee glanced at her watch. "In the thirty minutes since I've been home? No."

They'd spent another hour together, finishing Mark's white chocolate Easter bark, and there'd been no kissing or talk of kissing. They gave Mark all their attention. And it had been torture.

"You guys haven't even had your first date yet," Maddie said with a sigh. "It's so romantic. You've got so much ahead of you."

"Quit talking like an old married woman. You and Mick have only been together for three months."

But those were two more months than Maddie had ever been with a guy, and DeeDee would bet money this was the real thing. Anyone who'd seen them together could tell they had something special. Maddie's bush pilot had renovated the fishing lodge he'd been planning to sell and intended to reopen it for business come spring. DeeDee suspected Maddie would move out there with him.

Her sister, with her froufrou little dog, living on the edge of a lake in a cabin.

It had to be love.

"I think," Maddie began, but DeeDee's cell phone rang before she could finish.

DeeDee looked at the caller ID.

Jon.

She froze.

"Who is it?" Maddie asked.

"My... um... my agent." DeeDee got up, took her phone and her wineglass, and went to her bedroom. She let it ring a few more times, preparing herself.

"Jon," she said, cupping her hand around the device. "I didn't expect to hear from you again."

"Bygones," Jon said, as if it were nothing. "Got a deal for

you."

All professional. Nothing personal. Exactly how it should have stayed between them. DeeDee sank onto the bed, forcing herself to listen to Jon's words.

"Branding for a new tanning product. They like your look, want to run some test shots. It's a company out of Bridgeport, Connecticut. Imagine, your face on every cosmetic counter in the country. How does that sound?"

DeeDee's heart caught in her throat. Her face, everywhere. Two months ago, she'd have given her eye teeth for a chance like this. It was the sort of exposure that could reinvent her as a model and lead to bigger, better things. Not to mention, the residuals could carry over for years if Jon negotiated favorable terms.

"Are you listening?" Jon exhaled loudly.

"Yeah... yes," DeeDee said, feeling faint.

"There's only one catch. I told them you're on hiatus right now. They think you're recovering from a nose job."

"They think... what? Why?"

"They're not crazy about the original, so I did not correct their assumption." His fake French accent, once so delightful to her, now struck her as Bronx with an unidentifiable pan-offensive pseudo-European overlay. DeeDee could almost smell the smoke from the tiny imported cigarettes he insisted on smoking. "There's still time to have the procedure and recover, with no one the wiser. I'll locate a surgeon and text you the appointment details. Where are you again? Mongolia? Do they have doctors there?"

Had he always honked like that when he laughed?

"Marietta, Montana. We have TV and penicillin and everything." It was one thing for DeeDee to diss her home town, but she didn't appreciate hearing others do it.

"If you say so. Listen, DeeDee. Either you're serious or you're not."

"I'm serious, I am. It's just… This is a lot of information to take in in such a short time. It's a great opportunity."

"Am I good or what?" Jon took an audible drag and exhaled loudly. "Listen, DeeDee. I know we've had our differences, but this is your chance. I suggest you take it."

THREE DAYS LATER, DeeDee walked into the stucco-and-wood-sided building containing Dr. Edelman's consulting offices. The only thing identifying it as a medical office was the small, elegantly lettered sign posted in the lawn between the parking lot and the entrance, along with similar window lettering on the front door. The angled roofline gave it a modern West Coast contemporary look, upscale but not intimidating. Professional and elegant enough to match their exorbitant fees, yet homey enough to make people believe they were among friends.

Isaac had already given her the day off because Portia's baby shower was that evening and the fashion show the next day. When she'd left the previous night, he'd been quiet, nodding his goodbye as if expecting her to disappear after the almost-kiss.

She still wasn't sure she wanted to go through with this, but if the only thing standing between her and her dream job was a minor cosmetic procedure, she owed it to herself to at least find out what was involved.

She hadn't told Maddie, already knowing what she would say. Neither of them had much pain tolerance, and a broken nose was exquisitely painful according to Chad, who'd been head-butted by a horse once. Eric had broken numerous body parts during his bull-riding career, and Mick still had fading scars from his own recent facial fracture. She shuddered, then pushed away her doubts. She was gathering intel today, nothing more.

DeeDee glanced at her reflection in the window. She'd pulled out her favorite outfit for the occasion, which was the silk pants she'd worn the first time she'd met Isaac and the wrap Mark said made her look like a rainbow.

She smiled at the memory, luxuriating in the sensation of wearing something other than jeans and a T-shirt again. When was the last time she'd worn not just a swipe of mascara and lip-gloss, but full makeup, from primer to lashes? When was the last time she'd styled her hair in something other than a ponytail?

She tapped a finger against the side of her nose. Would the improvements she sought be worth the pain she'd endure to get them?

She was tougher than everyone thought, though. Anyone who could handle the cutthroat world of New York fashion could certainly handle a little pain.

The familiar panicky desperation bubbled inside her again. She'd wasted so much time fooling around and now, here she was, with thirty peeking over the horizon, and she still hadn't figured out what to do with her life.

She pictured Mark in the kitchen, dropping candies onto melted chocolate, looking up at her with glee.

Of Isaac, watching from the sidelines, his eyes following her movements. His appreciation. His admiration.

So what—was she going to give up modeling to work with handicapped people? Talk about a change.

No. This was who she was.

She straightened her shoulders and pushed through the doors.

"Good afternoon and welcome." The stunningly beautiful receptionist—Heidi, according to the nameplate on the desk—smiled, a bland, generic movement that didn't touch her eyes. "Is this your first time here?"

"Yup." DeeDee's smile felt like a rictus of terror. "Have you had Botox? I love how smooth your forehead is. I got one injection from my dentist when I was modeling in New York City because apparently, I have a line coming right here." She pointed to the left side of her mouth, aware that she was babbling again, but unable to stop it. "Mistake. I drooled in my sleep for three months."

Heidi's eyes widened, but her eyebrows still didn't move. Impressive. "I'll need you to fill out this form, please."

DeeDee gave her the necessary information and took a seat in the waiting room. The decor was spectacular, the walls a soft grey with pink undertones, the couches black leather with white throw cushions. The effect made her think of thick, fluffy slippers and curling up under a blanket on a cold night.

Even Heidi's blouse was a coordinating shade of pinkish-grey.

This was the place to have work done, if the interior design was anything to go by.

Which even she knew was not the way to judge a surgeon. But the branding was excellent, which meant he was smart.

"Deirdre Cash, Dr. Edelman will see you now." Heidi got to her feet and gestured for DeeDee to follow. Heidi's white pencil skirt matched the throw cushions. Again, DeeDee was impressed. No muffin top. No panty line. If Heidi was a creation of Dr. Edelman, they ought to be using her in their advertising.

Then again, having her sit out front, the face of the practice so to speak, was a kind of advertising.

The same way her feet advertised the Callus Palace?

Ugh.

Heidi held the door for her, and she walked into a spacious examination room. A white-sheeted table with a mattress three times thicker than the average doctor's, sat discreetly against the far wall. There were two full-length mirrors in the corner, for that dressing-room effect. People could see their front and back at the same time. There was also another mirror on wheels.

On the polished maple desk stood an oversized laptop, a professional-grade lamp, and another mirror.

No questioning what people were here to discuss with this doctor.

Isaac's words echoed in her ears.

You're more than what you look like. It's what a person does that matters.

Easy for him to say.

In her world, looks mattered a whole hell of a lot. Her appearance was everything. And being pretty was not enough. She had to be better than pretty.

She had to be perfect.

A second door at the back of the office opened, and the doctor entered the room.

"Hello, Ms. Cash. I'm Dr. Edelman. Pleased to meet you."

He was the single most beautiful specimen of a man she'd ever seen. No white coat or green surgical scrubs for him, at least, not for a consult. He wore a suit obviously tailored to his physique, which was no doubt built in a gym. He had an evenly sun-kissed complexion that she recognized was fake, but she didn't care. Just the right amount of wave to his blond-streaked hair. Sparkling blue eyes, chiseled cheekbones, a perfect jawline, and a few smile lines at the corners of his eyes.

Men could get away with smile lines. Must be nice.

He held out his hand, and they shook. His grip was firm and cool, his fingers strong. Even his voice was gorgeous, as if he'd had vocal coaching.

"You have lovely features." Dr. Edelman smiled at her. "I understand you're a model?"

"Yes." DeeDee tipped her head, waiting for the thrill the words had always caused. "I'm currently on a break, but would like to get back into it."

But the pride felt false. Small and misplaced.

Nor did she trust the doctor's admiration. It wasn't a compliment; it was an objective evaluation of a product that wasn't up to standard and may have to be recalled.

He didn't know her, after all. To him, she could be a photograph in a magazine.

"I understand you'd like to discuss rhinoplasty," he said. "Let's have a look."

He instructed her to lean forward, turn this way and that, and to close her eyes while he trained the high-powered lamp on her features for a better look. He took digital photographs from all angles, then uploaded them to the computer on his desk.

"I can see why you're looking to have this issue addressed," the doctor said when he was finished. "The imperfection, while small, detracts from the overall symmetry of your bone structure. It might not be noticeable to the average person, but you'll always be fighting the camera unless we correct it."

He pointed out the tiny bump that had relegated her to spots in hardware catalogs and flyers for podiatrists. "Let me do a mock-up of how it will look after the procedure." Dr. Edelman entered a few measurements, then showed DeeDee her face without the bump.

It looked almost the same.

She was disappointed that the effect wouldn't be more noticeable, which was ridiculous. She wanted people to believe that she was born this way, after all.

"Now." He leaned back in his chair and crossed his hands. "Because of your profession, I have a few other suggestions, if I may."

Other suggestions? Her nose she could understand, but she'd never been told there were other problems with her face.

"Of course," she said.

Dr. Edelman went on to discuss sun damage, the line by her mouth that the dentist had already screwed up, chemical peels, forehead lifts, and on and on.

By the time he shook her hand and left the office, she was ready to cry.

She'd come in excited to become more beautiful. Instead, she'd been told about all her other imperfections. And now that she knew about them, she wouldn't be able to stop thinking about them.

She stopped at the reception desk to pay Heidi the consultation fee, then left the office.

When she got into her car, she sat for a few minutes, wondering which would be the bigger mistake. To have the surgery... or to not have the surgery.

You're already perfect, just as you are.

She put her head onto the steering wheel, knowing her makeup would be ruined, but let the tears come anyway.

Chapter Sixteen

DEEDEE GOT BACK to Marietta in plenty of time to put the final changes on the community center for Portia's baby shower that evening, grateful for the distraction.

She'd washed off the tear-ruined makeup, replacing it with a light touch of foundation and mascara, put her hair in a ponytail again, and changed into a pair of dark jeans, a soft cotton-blend sweater, and Maddie's pink suede boots. No more glamour today, thanks to Dr. Edelman. Simple, classic, and clean.

She felt... tarnished. Defective.

"Stop it," she ordered herself. This was a party, a celebration, and she wasn't going to let her own Dr. Dumbass ruin it.

She put her hands on her hips and surveyed the community center. The pots of colorful spring bulbs coordinated beautifully with the festive streamers and the huge banner Cynthia had created from the comfort of her laptop.

DeeDee wasn't sure who all would be coming, but she hoped for a good turnout. Sage wanted a huge show of support for her niece. DeeDee would do better than that.

She glanced at her cell phone to check the time. The food wasn't coming for half an hour. She had time to pop over to Isaac's to see if he'd changed his mind about bringing Mark to the shower. It would be a great chance for him to meet a few more people in a casual, fun setting.

And support Portia at the same time.

Sure, she could call. But she wanted to see him. *Them.* The appointment with the surgeon had left a bad taste in her mouth. Mark would make her smile, and she needed that.

She parked Maddie's car in front of Isaac's house and looked at her hands on the steering wheel for a few minutes.

"Be honest, DeeDee," she muttered. She was still thinking about the kiss that hadn't happened. If ever she needed one, it was now.

She walked up the steps, determined to be breezy and confident. Neediness didn't suit her.

She walked inside, listening. By the sound of the laugh-track, Mark was upstairs, watching TV. She nudged open the door to Isaac's office. He sat at his desk, his back facing the door, his dark hair deliciously rumpled, his white shirt untucked, his feet—oh lordy—bare.

"Hey," she said quietly, so as not to startle him. "Have you decided about going to the shower with me? It would be fun. You could use some fun."

Isaac turned to the sound of her voice, dragging his gaze from yet another stack of reports. It was a wonder the man's eyes hadn't changed to scaled-down eight-and-a-half-by-eleven rectangles. He took off his glasses and held them in his hand. Very professorial. He parted his lips and nibbled on one of the arms. He had lovely, lovely teeth.

DeeDee's stomach jumped, not in the painful clench she'd become accustomed to, but rather a glittery, shimmery sensation like she was about to buckle in for an exciting ride.

"Shower?" he said, sliding that slow, heavy-lidded gaze to her mouth. His tongue darted out to catch the arm of his glasses to gently bite down on the plastic-covered metal.

He wasn't looking at her as if he saw defects.

"I told you. It's tonight." She swallowed and flicked a lock of hair out of her eyes.

He lifted his eyebrows. "I think I'd have remembered you talking about a shower."

The way he was looking at her was doing fantastic things for her bruised ego. She stepped into the doorframe and leaned against it, bumping her hip out, emphasizing the length of her denim-clad legs and the comfortable sweater that still did nice things for her modest décolletage. "You should come. I promise, you'll have a good time."

He lifted his eyebrows.

"It would do you good to try something different, rather than staying in and staring at a screen all day and night," she added. "Plus, I think Mark could enjoy it."

She laughed at the look on his face.

"The baby shower, Ike. The one I'm organizing for

Sage's niece, remember? The more, the merrier. Well, the more people, the more presents, I should say. Portia could use the help. You'd be doing a good thing." She paused for breath. "I gather that Portia's been thrown for a loop with this pregnancy, and Sage is hoping that some fun, pampering, and excellent presents will lift her spirits. The party's tonight. I'm inviting you, though at the moment, I have no idea why. Is any of this ringing a bell?"

One side of his mouth tipped upward. Anyone who didn't know what to look for would have missed it. But she recognized it for what it was—a smile.

"A baby shower," he said. "You might have mentioned. You can understand my confusion."

The other side tipped up as well. He was positively grinning at her now.

She took a few steps into the room and perched herself on the arm of one of the ghastly chairs, leaning back slightly. "If we're flirting again, I should warn you. I'm very competitive. And I never lose."

His eyebrows went way up at that. He sat back in his great swivel chair behind that massive oak desk and folded his arms. "You're competitive, are you?"

She didn't take her eyes off his. She felt a million times better than she had a minute ago. "Very. How about that shower?"

Diamonds sparkled in his onyx gaze. "The way you say it makes me feel dirty."

She hadn't expected that. He'd spoken the words with his usual inflection, which was almost a monotone. So why was she shivering like he'd just run a hand up the back of her thigh?

Good thing she was holding onto a chair.

He'd given her exactly the affirmation she craved. Suddenly, that was raising alarm bells.

She didn't want to consider what that meant.

DeeDee stood up slowly, forcing her legs to work, to hold her as she came up to the front of his desk, shifted the stack of reports, and planted her palms on the empty surface.

Flirting, she could do. Best not to think about the rest.

She leaned forward until their heads were perhaps three feet apart.

"If you feel dirty, Isaac, then you should do something about it." She used her breathy Marilyn Monroe voice. "Do I make you sweaty? Is your heart pounding like you've just had a long run in the hot sun and all you want to do is strip off all your clothes and stand under a spray of cool water, feel it slip over your bare skin, refreshing you, making you come alive—"

He stood up, swept the reports off his desk, and pulled her across the polished oak into his lap. He cradled the back of her head, and then it was happening. He was kissing her, his mouth hard and hungry, wet and wild, sweet, salty, and certain.

His fingers threaded through her hair, pulling her close

and closer, as his tongue swept the inside of her mouth, demanding, claiming, conquering. Passion rose hot and wild in her to match his, but where she let hers loose, he kept his carefully contained, like a dangerous animal that could never be fully tamed. His other hand was dangerously close to the underside of her breast, moving up and down restlessly, exploring while holding her tightly against his body, but never quite reaching where she wanted him to go.

The kiss seemed to go on forever. His hoarse breathing matched her own, and his body pressed hard, hot, and insistent beneath her. Time seemed to stop. She didn't know where she was. She didn't know who she was, or why or when, and didn't care at all. All she knew was the soft firmness of his mouth, the taste of clear mountain water with an afternote of dark chocolate, the shivery feeling she got when he rubbed his lightly stubbled cheek against hers.

DEEDEE'S HANDS SCRAMBLED at the back of his head, her fingers threading through his hair. "We shouldn't be doing this," she whispered. "Mark could come down at any minute."

"Don't think about Mark," he murmured against her mouth.

She was right, though. It was a mistake to get involved with DeeDee. It was wrong on so many levels. She worked for him. She was leaving town as soon as she could. She'd break Mark's heart when she did.

But he couldn't stop himself.

"I've wanted to do this for so long." She nibbled on his earlobe, making his breath catch in his throat. "Don't tell me you haven't been thinking the same thing."

She slipped her warm hand down the collar of his shirt, scratching lightly on the skin in the center of his back, in the places where he could never reach. It was animalistic, erotic, and he never wanted her to stop.

"You're killing me, DeeDee."

Her body shook against him as laughter rippled through her. "Then I'm doing it right."

He grabbed her bottom, lifted her up, and set her down on the desk. She opened her knees to let him step up against her. He could take her right here, right now. He wanted her so badly. She was terrible for him. She made him lose his mind.

"Wait." He broke the kiss and put his forehead against hers. They were breathing as if they'd just run a marathon. "We can't do this, not here. Not now."

Not ever.

"Why not? Everything seems to be working as far as I can tell." She nudged him gently with her knee.

"Oh, everything's working just fine. And believe me, I want it." He inhaled, determined to be honest. "I want you. But it would be wrong to let this go further."

Her smile faded. Hurt came into her eyes, then snuffed

out, replaced by shiny blankness. "Why?"

Isaac thought about Mark's face when he'd explained their mother was going to be traveling with her new husband and that Mark would be moving into a neat place where he'd make lots of friends and have so many interesting things to do.

His disappointment when he'd learned that Jodi-Lyn wasn't going to become his sister, after all. How, both times, his eyes had grown shiny with tears. How he'd asked in a little-boy voice, "She doesn't love me anymore?"

It had nearly torn the heart out of Isaac's chest.

"Relationships haven't been good for Mark," he said finally.

"Far as I can see," DeeDee said, "I've got my legs wrapped around you, not him."

Yes, she did, thank God and everything that was holy, and he wanted nothing more but for her to stay there and continue this exploration.

But he needed her to understand.

He stepped back, gently removing her ankles from his thighs.

"He's been hurt pretty badly. He needs me to be, well, his. I owe him that."

He wondered if he'd ever get over the guilt he bore for how the woman he'd almost married had treated Mark. Jodi-Lyn had never shared Isaac's sense of responsibility for his brother. But then, she'd avoided Mark whenever possible, always busy when Mom invited them for dinner. Finally, she'd admitted she was uncomfortable around Mark. She didn't know what to do or say around him and frankly, she considered it a waste of time. Mark wouldn't care, she insisted. And if he did, he'd soon forget.

Isaac should have broken things off far sooner than he had.

But it wasn't until Mom got engaged that things had come to a head. Jodi-Lyn had flatly refused to entertain the thought of Mark living with them, even briefly. There were places, she said, where he'd be happy. With his own kind.

But Isaac knew those places. He'd seen the stained institutional walls, smelled the rank odor of warehoused residents, some of whom resisted bathing until forced. The group home had been bad enough. He'd already felt Mark's arms clinging to his neck, heard his cries, begging not to be left behind, promising to be good, to stay out of the way, to not annoy Jodi-Lyn.

"My ex-fiancée and I didn't see eye to eye on Mark. He's the reason we split up."

Jodi-Lyn had given him an ultimatum. He'd chosen his brother.

"So, you're going to live like a monk for the rest of your natural life?" DeeDee slid off the desk and adjusted her clothing. She sounded mad. He couldn't blame her. These were the cards life had dealt him. He was trying to make the best play he could. His hand, after all, was not nearly as bad as Mark's.

"He already feels abandoned by Mom. Even though that's not the case, it's how he perceives it. Then I let him think Jodi-Lyn was going to take me away. I can't let that happen again."

But she surprised him by walking up and laying one hand against his cheek, cupping his face gently. "That's a heavy burden. I wish I could change your mind, and I wish I could say I understood."

She moved closer then and set her lips gently on his, a chaste kiss that spoke of a kindness at odds with her some-times-brash behavior. Was it possible that he'd hurt her?

"Isaac? DeeDee?"

Mark.

Isaac pushed away from DeeDee and wiped his mouth with the back of his hand. Mark sounded like a herd of elephants most of the time; how had he snuck in without them hearing?

"What are you doing?" Mark's confusion quickly turned to anger. "Are you kissing? DeeDee's my friend. You can't kiss her! You can't kiss DeeDee! She's my friend. Mine, mine, *mine*."

Mark's shouts descended into incoherent wails. He kicked at the door and punched his fist against the wall. He was heading for a full-fledged meltdown of the kind Isaac hadn't seen since before coming to Marietta. Worse even than when he'd broken the bowl.

"Mark, it's not like that," he began.

But DeeDee pushed past him.

"Mark!" She snapped out the word, grabbing for his arm.

He flung her away, almost hitting her in the process.

Isaac tried to intervene, but DeeDee blocked him with her body.

She caught Mark's hands in hers, pulled him close, and then held him, pressing his head against hers. "Mark, it's okay." Her voice was softer now. "I'm here. I know you're scared, but I'm your friend. You're okay."

Weeping now, Mark sank onto the floor, as if his legs couldn't hold him. "I don' wanna go back. I wanna stay with Isaac."

DeeDee glanced at Isaac over Mark's head.

He shrugged helplessly. "Mark, of course you're going to stay with me."

"Nuh-uh." Mark shook his head. "Kissing makes people I love go away. Makes me go to the bad place."

Oh, God.

Guilt choked Isaac like a knife to the throat. Relationships, as he'd explained to DeeDee, had not been good for Mark. But hearing his theory confirmed so succinctly by Mark himself jammed the dagger deeper and twisted it. The group home had left indelible, traumatic memories, ones associated with loss.

"Isaac's not going anywhere and neither are you," Dee-Dee said. "Us kissing changes nothing."

Confusion washed over Mark's face again.

"I won't go to the bad place?" Mark's voice was small and pitiful. "You won't take Isaac away?"

Just when Isaac thought his heart couldn't break any more...

"No more bad place, ever." DeeDee stroked his hair. "I won't take Isaac away from you. He'll always be your brother."

"And you'll still be my friend and Isaac's friend, too?"

"I can be your friend and his friend at the same time. I've got lots of friends, honey."

"Jo-lin didn't like me. She said she did, but she lied."

DeeDee wrinkled her nose. "Then Jodi-Lyn was a dumbass, just like your doctor."

Mark looked up cautiously, tears still glinting on his cheeks. "You still love me? Even though you kiss Isaac?"

"I love you and Isaac both, honey. I'm sorry, but you're going to have to deal with that. Think you can manage?"

"Both at the same?"

DeeDee slanted a quick look at Isaac. "Same amount, yep, but in different ways. It's how it is, my friend. Now, you're strong and smart and capable of handling this. Okay? Hug?"

Mark tightened the bear-hug until DeeDee winced. "Can I go upstairs and watch TV?"

Isaac watched, unable to speak.

Deirdre Cash had just admitted that she loved him.

Him and Mark.

Both.

And she didn't even seem to realize it.

"If you want," DeeDee said. "But there's a party tonight. I'd love you to come along, but you need to put on clean clothes."

"A party?" Mark frowned and tucked his head into his shoulder. Then he brightened. "Like the close-show? Where Sara Maria wears fancy close and looks so pretty? I want to do the close-show!"

Not the fashion show again. Isaac looked at DeeDee. "We already discussed that."

She gave an innocent shrug. "Maybe he and Sara Maria saw each other at the day program again. I didn't encourage him, Isaac. I swear."

"I have new close," Mark said. "I could do the close show. With Sara Maria."

"One thing at a time," DeeDee said. "First, the party tonight. Right now, hurry and get changed."

Mark hustled off, sunny again.

Maybe he was being overprotective. Maybe he should let DeeDee put Mark in her show, after all.

Maybe he was underestimating Mark.

Maybe he was underestimating DeeDee.

Chapter Seventeen

DEEDEE AND HER big mouth. She'd been trying to smooth things over with Mark, that was all, but somehow, she'd ended up telling the boy she loved him. And then she'd gone and included Isaac.

She'd just said that she loved Mark and Isaac. Both.

The same amount. In different ways.

Was that the truth?

DeeDee had never been in love before. She'd been in lust many times. She'd been in admiration of many cars, hopeful of many Christmas and birthday gifts, willing to accept trips and jewelry and theatre tickets and nights on the town.

She'd had more than her fair share of boyfriends—affairs, she supposed she should call them now. But her heart had stayed untouched.

She knew that because this time, for the first time, it was different.

Her heart was involved.

Touched.

And the crazy thing was that she and Isaac hadn't even

gone out on a date. They weren't involved. She was his employee, for heaven's sake. So, they'd kissed. One wildly unforgettable time. A momentary lapse of judgement, maybe. Did Isaac regret it?

She certainly didn't. If anything, she wanted more.

She did not understand what was happening and thoroughly hoped she'd have a chance to figure it out before Isaac called her on it.

Or maybe, he'd just let it go, pretend it never happened. Sometimes, people said things in the heat of the moment that they wished they could reel back into their traitorous mouths.

Heck, DeeDee did it all the time.

But this was different. She'd used the L word.

Love.

Love spoke of promises and futures and commitment and shared values and goals. She and Isaac barely knew each other.

But in the time they'd spent together, instead of her usual modus operandi with men—dinners out, movies, dancing, parties, and yes, hot nights and mornings that felt vaguely sordid—she and Isaac talked. They argued. They made chocolate. They walked in the park. They'd discussed Mark and what was best for him.

She and Isaac connected in a way she'd never experienced with a man before. And he treated her like a person, a thinking, feeling person whose opinions mattered, even when they were diametrically opposed to his own.

He challenged her, and she challenged him.

Oh, God.

"What am I going to do about this?" she whispered into the empty car.

There was only one person to talk to. She pulled out her cell phone. "Maddie?" she said when her twin picked up. "How did you know when you were in love with Mick?"

On the other end, there was silence. Then, a peal of laughter. "I'm so happy!" Maddie yelled over the airwaves.

"No, no, no," DeeDee wailed. "This isn't good. This is terrible."

"We *are* talking about Isaac, aren't we?"

"Yes, of course. Who else?"

"I don't know. Have you decided what to do about New York?"

She had. Jon wasn't going to like it, but he was the least of her concerns.

"Interested in subletting your place?" she asked.

"Absolutely!" Maddie whooped again. "When did you finally figure it out?"

DeeDee nibbled the corner of her lip. "I'm not sure."

Maddie laughed again. "I've known it since the night Cynthia was in the hospital, Dee. You were so annoyed with him. You couldn't possibly be that mad at someone you didn't care about."

"It could have been the flowers," DeeDee responded

faintly. "It was a pretty nice bouquet."

"You're hilarious," Maddie said. "Listen, I'm showing a house right now. Can we talk later?"

"Wait. You're coming to Portia's shower, aren't you?"

Maddie's breath whooshed out. "Right. Of course. I'll see you there. Don't worry. It'll be great."

"You scared me there for a minute," DeeDee said. "The worst thing would be for no one to show up."

Chapter Eighteen

ISAAC STEPPED THROUGH the doors of the community center, wondering how soon he could leave without appearing rude. He'd always believed that baby showers were for women, but DeeDee had emphasized that there would be lots of other men in attendance and that he and Mark must come, because nothing was worse than a half-empty party room.

In Isaac's opinion, there were many, many things worse, including those plastic glasses decorated with baby booties.

"Look, Isaac." Mark's face split into a grin at the sight of the punchbowl in the corner. "Can I have some?"

"Maybe later, buddy." Mark would be spinning in circles for hours if he drank the neon-pink potion.

"There you are!" DeeDee approached them, a look of relief on her face. She gave Mark a hug before stepping back to face Isaac. "I wasn't sure you'd make it."

Was she still sizzling as much as he was from their kiss? She was in full party-planner mode, so it was hard to tell.

"I said we'd come, so here we are."

"And?" She gestured to the decorations. "What do you think? Nice, huh?"

A pink-and-blue banner stretched from one corner of the room to the other. It said *Welcome, Baby* in curlicue lettering. Rainbow-colored streamers looped to meet it, their tails trailing down along the wall. A chair sat beneath, decorated with more streamers, identifying it as being for the guest of honor. Pots of flowers sat here, there, and everywhere. A collage of black-and-white baby pictures Isaac guessed were of the mother-to-be was tacked onto the wall, next to a blown-up copy of a sonogram with a sign saying, *Like Mother, Like Baby.*

One table was stacked with food, tiny crust-less sandwiches and pastries from the bakery, platters of colorful fruit and cheese, an obscene assortment of Sage's chocolate, of course, and an enormous cake with still more good wishes written in frosting.

A pile of gifts teetered off to the side, beautifully wrapped and beribboned packages large and small.

Isaac added an envelope to the pile. "Very nice. You did all this?"

"I like pretty things, and I'm good at asking for stuff," DeeDee said. "Not much, as skills go, but they work. Mostly."

She gazed at him steadily, and something unspooled inside him. "DeeDee," he began.

"Hey, there's my girlfriend," Mark said. He pointed a

stubby finger at a pretty young woman who'd just arrived. "Her name is Sara Maria. She's very smart and funny and she's my girlfriend. Can I talk to her?"

According to DeeDee, for the autistic young woman to tolerate, let alone enjoy, Mark's company was a huge triumph for them both.

"How about you introduce us?" he suggested. He wasn't comfortable with the possible romantic element, but it was better than thinking about whatever was or was not going on between him and DeeDee.

"Yay!" Mark grabbed Isaac with one hand and DeeDee with the other. "Come on, come on."

The slender young woman stood in the corner beside a man whose features resembled her enough to suggest they were related.

"Hi, Sara Maria." Mark blushed.

Sara Maria blinked rapidly and tapped her hands at her sides. "Hi, Mark."

Mark looked up at Isaac. "This is my girlfriend. She makes pie. She's smart and special and pretty. Isn't she pretty?"

He certainly looked smitten.

"Very nice to meet you, Sara Maria." Isaac tipped his head, guessing she wouldn't want to shake hands.

The man next to her, however, extended his hand immediately. "Brant Willingham. Sara Maria's big brother. And this is Rosie Linn, my fiancée."

The woman blushed and glanced lovingly up at Brant.

"Rosie's a script writer, but she also works part time at the chocolate shop with Sage and Portia," DeeDee explained after exchanging greetings.

"Sara Maria works at the pie store." Mark gazed wistfully at her. "I wish I could work at the pie store."

Isaac's heart twisted. So much had been denied Mark in his life so far, yet he remained, at heart, so happy. So hopeful. And now, for the first time, he was having a taste of meaningful contribution, community, love, acceptance... thanks to DeeDee.

Before he could speak, she took his arm and dragged him away. "Isaac, I see Maddie and Mick. And Chad! Oh, their neighbors are here, too! This is great. Look at all the people. Sage will be so pleased."

The river of words and names seemed unstoppable. DeeDee seemed a bit manic, her eyes shining a little too brightly, her cheeks a little too flushed. She was trying hard to be friendly, but to Isaac's eye, it didn't seem entirely reciprocal.

Then again, with all her chatter, she wasn't giving people much opportunity to respond. A preemptive measure?

DeeDee tapped a dark-haired woman's shoulder, then stepped back. She appeared to be acquainted with everyone in the room. But there was caution in her greetings, and some of the responses she received were warmer than others.

Or maybe he was imagining it. It didn't seem to faze her,

at any rate.

"Mel, Leda, have you met Isaac Litton? He just moved here from Chicago. Maddie sold him his house." She pointed into the corner where Mark and Sara Maria were now sitting side by side. "That's his brother, Mark. Isaac, this is Melinda Sweet and Leda Anders."

Leda, the shorter of the two, gave him a big, bright smile with just enough bite to tell him not to underestimate her. Melinda, slightly softer looking, touched his arm with the easy familiarity so many people in the town had. He wasn't used to it. But he liked it.

"Leda's married to Chad's brother, Eric," Deirdre continued. "Mel and her husband Austin live next door to them, at Sweet Montana Farms. Oh! There's Maddie. Excuse me, I need to speak to her. Play nice, kiddos."

She disappeared, and Isaac smiled at the women. "There must be something special about the water in Marietta, Montana to produce so many lovely women."

The younger woman, Leda, gave a throaty laugh. "I guess we'll see about that tomorrow. DeeDee's got half the town taking a turn on the runway at her fashion show. You know, for a city boy, you sure flirt like a natural-born cowboy."

Melinda pulled him out of the way of someone carrying a tray of chocolates. "Austin and I are Chicago transplants, too," she said, "so we can't lay claim to the magic water, but you won't find better people anywhere on this planet. How are you settling in?"

"Good." He glanced over to where Deirdre was chatting up another group of people. "It was rough at first. Mark doesn't like change."

"I hear DeeDee's been a big help." Leda's wide-eyed comment was a bit too innocent.

Heat prickled his chest. "She is. Mark adores her."

"And you?" Leda persisted.

Isaac stared blankly at her for a second before warmth flooded his cheeks. "Oh, no. It's not like that. Deirdre works for me."

Leda gave a hoot of laughter. "I meant it looks like your brother adores you, too. Interesting, where you went with that. The Marietta water's famous for a lot of things, you should know."

Isaac looked around him, desperate for rescue.

"Quit torturing him, Leda." Maddie Cash appeared suddenly and squeezed his elbow. "Isaac and DeeDee are just friends. And I'm sure he's already figured out that she can be a challenge no matter what kind of relationship you have with her."

Isaac exhaled with relief, his cheeks puffing out momentarily. "You've got that right. But she's rather remarkable, too. I've been pleasantly surprised."

Maddie's eyebrows arched. "I'd like to mention, for no reason in particular, that Mick and I started out as a business relationship."

"And Mick didn't plan to stay either, did he?" Leda said.

"So, you never know, Isaac."

"I'm here for good," Isaac said. "I wouldn't uproot Mark again now that I've finally gotten him settled."

"You are." Leda pointed her finger at him. "But who knows where DeeDee will end up. Right, Maddie? She's not exactly a big fan of little Marietta. First chance she gets, she'll hightail it out of here again. So, it's just as well you keep things simple with her."

Maddie shot Leda a dirty look.

"What?" Leda returned the look. "What did I say?"

"People change, Leda," Maddie said.

The reminder echoed hollowly inside Isaac. Of course DeeDee had plans to leave. Whatever might be happening between them wouldn't change that, and why should it? He'd told her he was unavailable. He had no right to be disappointed. Mark, however, would be devastated. She knew him well enough by now to predict his reaction. How dare Deirdre let Mark get attached to her if she had never intended to stick around?

A hand touched his arm, and Maddie leaned toward him. "Don't listen to Leda," she whispered. "DeeDee thinks the only place she can shine is New York. But she's changing. Please don't say anything to her about this, okay? Give her a little time."

But before he could think about it anymore, someone gave a shrill whistle and the voices stilled.

"Welcome, everyone," DeeDee said from where she

stood on a chair at the front of the room. "I just got a call from Sage. She and Portia are about to arrive. As you all know, this is a surprise party, so everyone quiet now. I'll turn out the lights and when she opens the door, I'll turn them back on and we'll all yell surprise, okay?"

She put a finger to her lips to shush them all and hit the light switch.

How could she think that modeling was the only thing she was good at? Look at how she was managing this crowd. Look at the lovely party she'd put together, how thoughtful she'd been in arranging things just so for the young expectant mother.

A hush fell over the room. Then, footsteps. Light flooded the room, and they all jumped up.

"Surprise!"

Someone screamed. Portia, the guest of honor, stood in the doorway, one hand gripping the frame, the other on her rounded belly. Her face was leached of color, her eyes like pie plates.

Sage, DeeDee's chocolate-making friend, put her arm around Portia, staring at the crowd. The skin around her eyes tightened and her lips flattened into a thin line.

"DeeDee," Sage said. "A word."

DeeDee quickly joined the two at the door, and then, to Isaac's surprise, she clapped a hand over her mouth.

What was going on?

"Poor girl looked like she was going to faint," Maddie

said.

"Portia or DeeDee?"

"Both," she whispered back.

Sage bent over Portia, speaking low and earnestly to her, while DeeDee stepped back into the festive room. Her smile was tight and she was blinking too quickly. "Change of plan. We're going to take it down a notch. Talk amongst yourselves for a moment, okay?"

What had happened?

Portia straightened her shoulders and entered the room, still like a deer in the headlights, but with courage now. Sage stuck closely to her side.

There was no announcement this time, no shouts of surprise, no delighted exclamations. If Isaac had to guess, he'd say Portia looked torn between embarrassment, anxiety, and heartbreak.

But she bravely addressed the room.

"Thank you, everyone." She swallowed, her slender throat working with the effort. "This is… very kind."

She put a hand to her mouth, tears sparkling in her eyes.

"No presents if you cry," DeeDee said, looking very close to tears herself. "So enough with the waterworks already."

Her tone was apparently the right mix of tender and tough because Portia gave a wobbly smile and began making her way into the crowd. But first, she gave DeeDee a huge hug.

DEEDEE COULDN'T HAVE felt more horrible. She'd sent invitations out everywhere, thinking that the more people who came, the more gifts Portia would receive and the more supported she'd feel.

She'd used the list Sage had given her as a starting point, and then added every name she could think of, encouraging the women to bring husbands and boyfriends where applicable. Showers weren't hen parties anymore, after all.

Secretly, she wanted Isaac to be there, to witness her triumph.

It should have occurred to her that Portia, a pregnant woman without a partner, didn't want to be surrounded by couples.

Idiot. Thoughtless. Ditzy DeeDee, back at it.

Sage recovered quickly to be her usual gracious self, but DeeDee could tell she was disappointed that the party had been a big, distressing social event, rather than the small, intimate gathering she'd intended.

Awesome. She'd ruined another party. Wait until Cynthia heard. The fashion show was tomorrow and Cynthia was already stressed about it, though pretending she wasn't.

But she got her wish. Isaac was here, witnessing it all. DeeDee in her full glory, screwing up again.

Served her right.

Served *him* right, for that kiss.

Her heart twisted. It was such a great kiss.

"Something's wrong with that girl," said a crusty voice

that could only belong to Carol Bingley.

DeeDee's head whipped up.

The town gossip tipped her chin in Portia's direction. She'd had her fair share of fun at the Cash girls' expense over the years. Not that they hadn't given her reason to talk. But she and Maddie could take it.

DeeDee wasn't about to let Carol Bingley start bad mouthing Portia.

"Whatever do you mean?" she asked in a silky tone. The woman had no ability to read body language, or she'd know already that she'd poked the beehive.

"Look at her, all colly-wobbles because of a baby shower. If she's embarrassed about her condition, it's no one's fault but her own. There's only been one immaculate conception as far as I know, and it wasn't this one."

"Luckily," DeeDee said, biting the words off, "she's got the support of her family and friends."

"For what that's worth. Those Carrigan girls are all trouble." Carol Bingley shook her head. "I don't blame Hawksley. A widower, raising a pack of girls on his own. He did the best he could."

"Portia's a Bishop, not a Carrigan," DeeDee pointed out.

"Her mother's a Carrigan." Carol waved away the detail. "Blood always tells. I don't know why Sage is coddling her like this. If Portia's going to do this on her own, she needs to toughen up, the sooner, the better. Especially if there's something wrong with the baby. That aunt of hers had one with mental defects, after all. Maybe it runs in the family."

Isaac had joined her just in time to hear this part of Carol's rant, and DeeDee saw him stiffen at her words.

She put up a hand to keep him from talking. She had this, cold.

"Dani Carrigan's daughter has Down syndrome. There's a young man over by the door with Down syndrome, too. His name is Mark. Sara Maria, the girl with him, is autistic. That cute kid standing by the food table is Jade. She has Asperger's syndrome. You'll want to watch what you say about people with special needs."

"Oh, I know, everyone's special these days," Carol said. "But no one hopes for an abnormal child. If it has problems, I don't know how Portia will cope, an unwed mother as she is. Even if her baby is normal—"

"Normal like who?" DeeDee lowered her voice. "You? I hope not."

Carol's lips tightened. "No one would blame her for putting it up for adoption. Which makes you wonder why we're having a party—"

DeeDee grabbed Carol's elbow and yanked her toward the door. "This," she said, "is a happy event. You and your opinions aren't welcome here. Now, get out."

She shoved her through the door and closed it behind her, barely managing to resist kicking it.

"Well, well," Isaac said. He was standing close enough that his body heat tugged at her like a force field. "Look who's standing up for the underdogs of the world."

"The woman's an ass. It was long overdue. Sorry you had to hear that."

Isaac gave her a long, slow look. "I'm not. You are amazing, Deirdre Cash."

Tears prickled at the backs of her eyes. "No, Isaac," she said. "I'm really not."

"You are." He touched her arm. "And while I've got you here, I'd like to tell you I've changed my mind."

Dread filled her, twisting her stomach again. "I'm kind of maxed-out on bad news, Isaac. If you're going to fire me, please wait until after tomorrow. If you're regretting that kiss, we can pretend it didn't happen."

He lifted his hand to her cheek, brushing away a tear. His touch was so gentle that it made her eyes well up again. "Nothing like that. I just wanted to say that if Mark still wants to be in your show, it's okay with me."

She barely managed not to leap into his arms. He hadn't mentioned the kiss, her awkward declaration, the weird place they'd entered.

She didn't know what that meant.

But he was still being lovely.

Chapter Nineteen

LESS THAN TWELVE hours later, the community center was transformed for the show. The potted flowers from the shower were doing double duty, with the bulbs going to Cynthia and Sage for planting after everything was done. They'd offered them to Portia, but she insisted they keep them as she didn't have the time, energy, or permanence for gardening.

She'd been gracious about the baby shower. DeeDee had been right about one thing, at least. Portia *had* cleaned up on the presents front. She'd be writing thank-you notes for weeks. Her tremulous gratitude had been touching to see.

Every time Portia alluded to her uncertain future, Dee-Dee wanted to cry. The unconscious way the quiet woman stroked her belly spoke of love, but her eyes were haunted, her excitement muted with caution.

Whatever her secrets, she wasn't sharing.

DeeDee shook off the thoughts. If she should be worrying about any pregnant woman, it should be Cynthia, anyway. This fundraiser reflected on Cynthia's company, so

DeeDee was determined to make it the best fundraiser Marietta had ever seen.

She gave a little wave to where Cynthia sat in a wheelchair next to the aisle. She'd been allowed to attend the event on the condition she restrict her enthusiasm to a queen-like wave. Mom, Norm, Chad, Maddie, and about a dozen other people hovered around, making sure she stayed calm.

If only DeeDee had someone to keep her calm.

Isaac would work.

No, Isaac would only make things worse.

She huddled just behind the curtain separating the changing area from the runway and forced herself to focus.

She could worry about Isaac later.

For now, the show must go on. It was a mock-up affair, of course, created by adding a sturdy length of sheet-covered two-by-fours and plywood that extended from the center of the stage, into the audience.

The town had come out in force, she was relieved to note, hoping the models wouldn't get nervous because of the crowd. Isaac was sitting near the front, his eyes glued to the curtain, his expression tight, worried. No small talk for him.

She'd been shocked and delighted that he'd allowed Mark to participate, after all.

She hoped he wouldn't distract Mark.

She wished he wasn't distracting her.

It was time to start. She glanced at her watch, then at Eric and Chad Anders, standing in the wings. Chad lifted one finger for her to wait while a small chattering group found their seats.

She was pleased that the brothers, founders of Building Tomorrow and strong supporters of Logan Stafford's program, had agreed to assist her at the mic. Their down-home sexy good looks always attracted attention and would ensure generous donations.

The lights dimmed. Chad gave her the all-clear, plus a huge, supportive smile, and she stepped out into the spot-light.

"Good afternoon everyone," she said.

The crowd, already quietening, grew still. So many eyes on her. Stage fright, that long-vanquished enemy, chuckled evilly at the back of her mind. She'd spent so many hours in front of an audience, having critical eyes on her, but they'd always been looking at the clothing, the product, or assessing her movement or features.

They'd never been looking at her. As a person.

She cleared her throat and lifted the mic.

"Welcome to Marietta Style," she said, "a fashion show dedicated to real people who wear real clothes."

The applause was polite, but sincere, and she took courage from the smiling faces.

"Most of the outfits you'll see tonight have been provided by Sandra Reynolds of Copper Mountain Chic, who truly brings style to Marietta. The mouthwatering treats in front of you are compliments of Sage Carrigan of Copper Mountain Chocolates, and we have Emerson Moore and Clifford Yerks of Two Old Goats Wine store to thank for the delicious beverages. And, of course, that we're here at all tonight is thanks to Cynthia Henley, of CH Solutions, who orchestrated the entire event for Building Tomorrow. Marietta is lucky to have so much talent among us."

She turned to acknowledge the donors, who half-stood and waved to polite applause, then returned to her seat. Cynthia waved from her wheelchair.

"Human beings are social creatures," DeeDee continued, making sure to include the bullet points Chad had given her. "We all have a need to contribute to our world in some way. But for people with developmental disabilities, this can be difficult. We often don't know how to interact with those who are different from us, and it's all too easy to distance ourselves from those who make us uncomfortable. But studies have shown that society as a whole benefits when we embrace our differences."

A round of polite applause greeted this remark.

"We have many differently abled people in our community, including my friend Mark Litton who you'll meet shortly. Mark has Down syndrome and lives with his brother, Isaac."

She sent a quick smile in Isaac's direction, but he did not return it, his gaze intense, wary. He was nervous for Mark, of course.

Keep smiling, just keep smiling.

"Mark and Isaac came to Marietta because they recognized a good, kind place where people are valued regardless of differences. Recently, Mark has been spending time at Anders Run, where he's enjoyed learning some new skills and helping with Chad's woodworking projects, thanks to the guidance of Logan Stafford. Logan, with the support of Eric and Chad Anders of Building Tomorrow, hopes to make this kind of partnership available to other people with disabilities, providing personalized occupational plans to enrich their lives and help them reach their full potential."

The crowd was listening intently, and the faces she could see were open and encouraging.

She risked another glance at Isaac, but this time, his chilly mask slipped, revealing so much emotion that it stole her breath away. Hope shone from his eyes, along with fear and sadness and gratitude. Suddenly, DeeDee realized how much trust he'd placed in her by allowing her into their lives. She knew he wanted Mark to be challenged, to grow, to succeed on his own merits. Yet, he also wanted to protect him from pain.

Isaac's love was fierce and unshakeable. Dangerous.

Mark was so lucky to have him.

Anyone would be.

DeeDee cleared her throat, then swallowed as Eric Anders joined her on stage. "There is a table at the back outlining the initiative proposed by Building Tomorrow. Halfway through our show, there will be a twenty-minute intermission, during which I encourage you to look over the table and pledge your support for personalized programs for developmentally disabled adults in Marietta. Now, let's enjoy Marietta Style!"

She handed the mic to Eric.

"Folks, let's hear it for our own fashion maven and coordinator of this event, Deirdre Cash," Eric said as applause rolled through the crowd. "DeeDee has curated the best catwalk looks that will most influence your wardrobe choices this year—for women and men, kids and teens, many of whom you will recognize today."

More applause. DeeDee tipped her head to the audience and blew kisses of thanks, then slipped offstage, grateful for the many residents who'd agreed to participate. She'd forgotten how generous Marietta could be. Had they always been this way?

Perhaps, having written the town off and set her sights elsewhere, she'd never opened herself to the acceptance that had always been here, waiting.

Melinda Sweet, the first model to take to the stage, clutched DeeDee's arm. "I'm so nervous. How do I look?"

DeeDee gripped Mel's shoulders and looked firmly into her eyes. "You look fabulous. Unbelievable. This is your moment to shine, understand?"

From behind the curtain, they heard Eric say, "The cold-shoulder trend remains huge. Rucksacks are the bag to be seen with and prairie is the new boho."

"That's your cue." She gave Mel a nudge.

"I can't believe you talked me into this," Mel whispered over her shoulder as she slipped through the curtain.

"Add some originality to your wardrobe with this unique asymmetric sweater in iced mocha." Eric read Deirdre's words smoothly. "Crafted from a cashmere-like fabric, it features long sleeves, a mock neck, and a side slit, perfect for the still-cool nights of spring. Paired with seriously stretchy faux-suede leggings and short stack-heeled boots, this outfit brings comfort to flair, perfect for the office, lunch with a friend, or a shopping spree."

Mel completed the end and both sides of the runway, pausing to cock a hip as directed, then returned behind the curtains.

"Whew," she said, whipping the drape closed behind her. "I did it. That was actually kind of fun."

"There'll be time to talk after." DeeDee zipped up the back of Maddie's dress, handed Mel another outfit, then turned to Sara Maria, who stood motionless at the entrance to the runway.

Oh, no. Sara Maria had begun to come into her own when her pie-baking skills earned her a job at the local bakery, but it was clear that her comfort level was stretched thin with this event. Maybe DeeDee should have scheduled her for later in the program. But too much waiting and the girl might back out.

"You can do it, Sara Maria." DeeDee held out a hand,

but didn't touch her.

"He hasn't said the words yet. The 'lovely young woman' part."

They'd practiced this. Sara Maria needed the cue to go exactly as planned. Eric knew this.

"It's okay. He'll say them. Just wait." DeeDee peered around the corner, listening for the patter, but Eric had strayed from her notes.

"Aren't we lucky to have so many good-looking people in our town?" he was saying as Maddie finished her turn on stage.

More appreciation from the crowd. Eric knew how to work a room, which was great. But if he didn't stick to the script, the girl wouldn't walk.

"I understand that Sara Maria Willingham is modeling a must-have for the season," he said, returning to the script. "A lovely outfit worn by a lovely young woman."

DeeDee whooshed out a breath. "Okay, there it is. Go!"

Sara Maria stepped through the curtains on her own.

"This printed poncho," Eric read, "is made of a whisper-soft angora blend and can be worn as a light coat or as an extra layer for a stylish outfit."

Sara Maria marched to the end, stopped, then did the same at both sides of the T-shaped platform. No smile, no pose, no frills. DeeDee had asked her to walk a certain path, wearing certain clothing, and that was what she did.

It was perfect.

DeeDee could see Brant Willingham, Sara Maria's older brother and guardian, cheering and waving from the front row. She wondered if Isaac and Brant had ever traded stories about life with their special siblings. Maybe she'd suggest they start a resource group for family members.

"Isn't Sara Maria pretty, DeeDee?" Behind her stood Mark, bouncing on the balls of his feet. "She's my girlfriend. Sara Maria makes delicious pie and she is my girlfriend."

"She's very pretty, Mark. Can you tell me what I said about you staying in line, so we don't get confused?"

He pursed his lips and scrunched his eyebrows. "I need to stay in line so we don't get confused."

"Right." She nudged him gently back to his spot.

"Nice job, Sara Maria." Maddie, next in line, grinned at the girl as they passed.

Sara Maria continued to the changing area, no doubt eager to return to her own clothing.

Maddie had no trouble being in front of a crowd, but DeeDee had carefully chosen a pair of low-heeled ankle boots for her outfit. If anyone was likely to wipe out today, it would be Maddie, as she'd already broken one ankle in her life.

Maddie came back and switched places with Dakota Parker. DeeDee had dressed her in a printed blouse in pomegranate that had front pockets, a buttoned neckline, and roll-tab sleeves.

"I'm doing this for Mr. Fluffy Legs," Dakota said.

DeeDee had agreed to adopt the cat in return for Dakota's participation. She couldn't bear the thought of someone else adopting the animal and breaking Mark's heart.

"As soon as Clementine moves out, he moves in, I promise. You look gorgeous, by the way. Bryce is going to lose his mind when he sees you."

Dakota blushed and tipped her chin. She had it bad. Her relationship with Bryce was still new, but anyone who saw them together could tell it was going to last.

It was so cute.

"I've seen the outfit you're modeling," Dakota said. "I think Isaac Litton's going to go a little crazy tonight, too."

DeeDee swallowed a cough. "Isaac? He's here to cheer for Mark. And to support a worthy cause. That's all."

She knew her feelings, but she didn't know his.

A snort of laughter sounded behind her. She looked over her shoulder to see Mel and Maddie, listening.

"Isaac's tongue will be on the floor," Maddie said.

Mel laughed. "There will be a lot of people in that state tonight. You're brilliant, DeeDee, in using ordinary people as models. As nerve-wracking as it is, I caught Austin's eye in the crowd as I was sashaying down the catwalk and let me just say, I'm glad Abel's staying with his grandmother tonight."

ISAAC SAT IN the chair DeeDee had designated for him, near

Mick, Cynthia, and Chad, when he wasn't on stage.

Austin Sweet, from the honey farm next to Anders Run, sat with Logan Stafford in the row behind them. Their wives, Isaac had been told, were participating in the show, and would join them in the audience when their turns were over.

"Are we allowed to eat the chocolate?" Mick asked, reaching for the plate. "I hope there are lots of salted caramels."

"I requested them with you in mind," Cynthia said. "But you'll have to try the Easter Egg Bark, too. Isn't it pretty? It's a special item Sage created this year. I think it'll be a huge hit."

It was a fancier version of the white chocolate bark Dee-Dee had made with Mark.

"It's delicious," Isaac said. "DeeDee made a batch of it with my brother."

Was that the moment he'd fallen in love with her?

It had begun without him noticing, he realized. A million tiny things had made him care for her. The way she put her hands on her hips when she spoke to Mark, affectionate and bossy at the same time. How she persisted, despite Mark's whining and Isaac's negativity, to bring freshness and energy to their home. How she'd put a piece of chocolate on his tongue and made him taste it, really taste it, find the pleasure he'd been too busy or too preoccupied to notice.

How she was as comfortable and confident in jeans and

no makeup as she was decked out in her finest.

"I hear she gave Carol Bingley the boot yesterday," Cynthia said. "I wish I'd seen it. It's all anyone's talking about. DeeDee the defender. I'm not surprised. She's done the same for me. She and Maddie both. I'm so lucky to have them as my sisters."

Cynthia was speaking rather pointedly to him.

"Mark and I are lucky, too," he responded.

But for how long? DeeDee never talked about her future, and he had the impression she was still undecided, waiting for something, especially after what Leda had said.

On the other hand, what about her comment about loving them? Was it a casual remark or did it mean something?

As if on cue, the curtains at the end of the stage shifted and there she was, modeling a brand-new outfit. He barely heard Eric's words, so taken was he with the vision she presented. She moved with a poise and grace not always evident in her day-to-day life, surveying the crowd regally, making eye contact, her lips curved upward softly.

In truth, Isaac had been mesmerized since the moment DeeDee had first taken the mic to introduce the show. He'd known she was beautiful, of course, but he'd never have guessed her to be such an excellent public speaker. There was passion in her words and gestures.

Passion on behalf of Mark.

Did she even know how incredible she was?

Of course not. She'd been focused on her failings for so

long that she'd lost sight of who she really was.

The irony.

This time, the applause was more than polite.

Maddie leaned over Mick and tapped Isaac on the leg. "DeeDee's great, isn't she?"

He nodded, wondering what DeeDee had told her sister about him. About them. If there even was a them.

The lights dimmed and the music began, an upbeat big-band-style piece that caught everyone's attention.

A small arm shoved aside the curtain, and a girl he guessed to be around nine or ten jumped out.

At the sidelines, DeeDee took the mic from Eric. "Please welcome Savannah Dawson, who loves soccer, chocolate, and her little brother. Savannah's lovely brushed-cotton pinafore in peach floral is the perfect outfit for a spring outing with the grandparents. Thank you, Savannah."

The girl curtsied to a wave of laughter and more applause.

"Next, we have Melinda Sweet again. This busy nurse-midwife is wearing a jersey-knit sheath that combines comfort with elegance."

Behind Isaac, Austin Sweet got to his feet, whistling and cheering as his wife waltzed down the runway. She paused at the end nearest them and blew a kiss.

DeeDee described the outfit, which looked like a green dress to Isaac, and then it was time for the next model.

Dakota Parker, the woman from the animal shelter, was

followed by her sister, Nevada, then a couple of men he hadn't met yet, then two friends of Mark's from the May Bell program. Lastly, an elderly couple strode out hand in hand.

Logan got to his feet. "That's my cue," he whispered.

He edged past the people sitting in the row and took the mic from DeeDee, who disappeared into the shadows behind the stage.

The music changed as a teenage boy stepped onto the runway. He glanced up at Logan, blinking in the bright lights.

"Please welcome our next model," Logan said, nodding to the boy. "Carter Boyd, a recent graduate of Marietta High, apprenticed with me in the Building Tomorrow program. Now he works at Big Z Hardware in the lumber department and has a promising future in construction."

Chad leaned in. "That kid would never have made it through school without Staff."

Isaac had heard about 'Logan's kids' as they were called, the ones who helped with his heritage house restoration projects, students who weren't succeeding in the academic setting, but thrived with a less-traditional approach.

Logan's passion reaffirmed Isaac's decision to settle here with Mark. That the entire town would come out to support this fundraiser was icing on the cake. That DeeDee had pulled all the myriad details of this show together proved to him that not only did she have more friends in Marietta than she believed, but that she also vastly underestimated her own talents.

Carter clumped in his sparkling-new work boots to each end of the runway, and then practically ran back to the curtain.

"Next," Logan said, "we have someone else I'm very proud of—my daughter Jade."

The child walked out stiffly, her brow furrowed. Her sleek dark hair and eyes hinted at her Asian heritage, but the tilt of her head and the tightness of her shoulders gave evidence that she, like Sara Maria, was on the Autism spectrum.

She didn't look happy to be there, but there was no questioning her determination.

Maddie, back in the audience now that her stint onstage was done, leaned over again. "Jade is Samara's daughter from her first marriage. Logan's in the process of adopting her. They're trying to decide what to do about her name. Right now, she's Jade Davis-Kim-Stafford, which is a mouthful for anyone, let alone a kid."

"Jade loves ice cream, bike riding, and her service dog Bob," Logan went on, "who is part Labrador and part Border Collie."

"And part luck of the draw," Jade added, frowning fiercely. "Bob is a girl. Bob is my dog."

Laughter rumbled over the crowd.

"Bob is definitely Jade's dog," Logan confirmed. "Jade is

wearing dark-wash blue jeans and a three-quarter sleeve cotton-blend shirt. Thank you, Jade."

More applause.

Isaac admired the camaraderie he sensed among these people. Would he and Mark truly be able to be a part of something like this?

Another music change.

"Next up is Mark Litton, the young man DeeDee mentioned in her opening."

Isaac sat up straight, his breath quickening.

Mark stepped through the curtain. Isaac could see Dee-Dee in the wings, urging him on. A hush fell over the crowd, followed by oohs and aahs.

DeeDee had dressed Mark in a tuxedo, complete with bow tie, shoes polished to a mirror-like shine, and neatly cut hair styled to perfection.

He looked so proud of himself, so handsome, so... smart. Isaac had to admit his brother didn't look uncomfortable or embarrassed. If anything, he looked confident, like he was having fun.

He looked, Isaac realized, normal.

A stab of guilt ran through him. DeeDee had accused him of not pushing Mark hard enough, of treating him differently, letting him fit the stereotype of people with Down syndrome, instead of emphasizing his uniqueness and his strengths.

"Mark is wearing a white double-breasted shirt and a

three-piece charcoal penguin suit. Thank you, Mark."

Mark went to do another pirouette. But this time, his foot slipped as he began the turn.

Isaac's heart lodged in his throat.

You had to get cocky.

Everything happened then as if in silent, slow motion.

Mark's arms reached into the air, the triumphant grin fading, replaced by wide, frightened eyes and a mouth open in a big O. The shiny shoes slid on the smooth surface of the runway and his legs went sideways, angling toward the far wall, the crease of his slacks rippling like water.

Mark landed with a thump that reverberated throughout the building. One of his shoes flew off into the crowd. His new glasses bounced off his nose and clattered to the other side of the runway.

In his peripheral vision, Isaac saw DeeDee leap out from between the curtains, clutching the edges of a terry-cloth robe to her chest, her hair clipped up away from her face.

Isaac had barely gotten to the end of his row before DeeDee was at Mark's side.

"Mark, honey, are you okay?" he heard her ask. DeeDee put her arm around his shoulders to help him sit up.

Appearing winded, Mark nodded and blinked. Isaac could see tears sparkling in his eyes.

"I sorry, DeeDee." His voice wobbled, a warning sign of what was coming next. Isaac made it to the edge of the stage and gestured to Mark, vividly aware of the audience watching everything.

DeeDee gestured to Logan. A moment later, the spot-light went off, the room lights came on, and the ambient music began again. Thank God.

"We're going to take a short pit stop, everyone," Logan announced. "It's time for chocolate."

"Where are his own clothes?" Isaac muttered. "I'm taking him home."

"No, you can't." DeeDee gazed at him in dismay.

"I wanna go home," Mark said in a hitching voice.

His heart broke for Mark's humiliation. In the wake of that pain, anger rode in. "He just fell on his ass in front of a roomful of people. It's not a shining moment."

DeeDee looked at him, then very deliberately squatted down to sit cross-legged on the stage beside Mark, tugging the robe over her bare legs. "Mark. Are you hurt? Did you hit your head?"

Mark snuffled and leaned against her. "No. Only my butt. And, DeeDee, I lost a shoe."

She gave him a tight side-hug. "It's right here. Let me help you put it back on."

"Forget the shoe," Isaac said.

DeeDee ignored him. She took Mark's chin in her hand and looked directly at him. "Mark, the only way to handle this is to get back on your feet and finish it. Are you brave enough for that?"

"Deirdre," Isaac began.

She turned the force of her gaze on him then. "He can do this, Isaac. Trust me. Trust him."

She gave Mark another squeeze. "Do what I do, okay, honey? It's going to be okay. Isaac, please take your seat."

She gestured again to Logan as Isaac reluctantly went back to his chair. He'd spent so many years fighting Mark's battles because someone had to stick up for him. But had his well-meant protection kept his brother from discovering his own inner strength?

The room lights dimmed and the spotlight illuminated Mark, looking slightly rumpled, and DeeDee, a barefoot princess in a bathrobe, her head held high, a confident smile on her beautiful face.

"Ladies and gentlemen," Logan said, "Mark Litton and Deirdre Cash."

DeeDee took Mark's hand and raised it in the air, like a prizefighter after a winning match.

There were still remnants of tears shining on Mark's face, but he was watching DeeDee carefully. He wiped his cheeks with his free hand and glanced cautiously at the crowd.

Then, to everyone's shock, DeeDee lifted her other hand and gave a whoop. Mark jumped and tried to take a step back, but DeeDee pulled him closer.

"Everyone falls," she shouted. "It's the ones who get back up who are the winners."

Mark smiled hesitantly, his eyes on DeeDee. Then he lifted his other hand and gave a yell, too. Then a second one.

She wasn't trying to torment Mark, Isaac realized. She was helping him grow. And Mark could handle it, after all.

"This is what it's all about, people," Logan said as people leaped to their feet, clapping and cheering. "Helping each other up when we fall."

DeeDee looked at him from across the room. She tapped the side of her nose and gave him a smile of such sweetness that it was as if the crowd around them evaporated, leaving them alone together, their feelings exposed, as readable as if they were inches apart, holding hands.

DeeDee pretended not to care about people because it hurt too much to be rejected. She didn't wear her heart on her sleeve, like Mark did. But to Isaac, she might as well have. That perfect glittery exterior hid a soft, warm heart as vulnerable as anyone else's.

Jodi-Lyn claimed to love Isaac, but she wouldn't even change dinner plans to accommodate Mark.

What had DeeDee said? She loved them both. The same amount, but in different ways.

She loved them.

Both.

If that wasn't a relationship, he didn't know what was.

Chapter Twenty

CHAD ANDERS WAITED quietly at the podium, allowing the crowd to chatter for a few minutes while DeeDee and Mark left the stage. A few minutes later, Mark thundered down the side steps to join Isaac in the audience.

"You did great, buddy." Isaac squeezed his brother's arm.

"People cheered, Isaac!" Mark's face was aglow. "I fell and people cheered. I didn't throw up."

"I knew you could do it." Though he'd needed convincing.

The music changed again, as did the lights.

Isaac sat up. It must be DeeDee's turn.

"She's played the role of emcee," Chad said in a grand voice. "She's stage managed the models, she's arranged clothing, fussed with hair, even modeled her bathrobe for us. She's handled the decorations, the donations, every practical detail down to the water bottles for the models. And she's done it all for the sake of her sister, Cynthia Henley, my soon-to-be wife and the soon-to-be mother of my child."

Chad's voice caught. Any remaining chatter fell silent.

"Deirdre Cash is not only beautiful and talented," he continued when he could, "but she's also got a heart as big as the Montana sky. Please welcome our final model, a huge supporter for Building Tomorrow and the true star of Marietta Style, my friend, and almost-sister, our own DeeDee Cash."

The applause was deafening.

"Whoo-hoo," Mark yelled beside him. "DeeDee, Isaac. DeeDee!"

When she burst through the curtain, one arm extended, her shoulders back, her chin high, Isaac almost didn't recognize her.

Her caramel-streaked hair was caught up in some elaborate twist that sparkled in the lights. Long, dark eyelashes swept over creamy skin, her cheekbones and jaw as elegant as lines of music.

She was DeeDee… but not the version he'd grown familiar with. This was a glittering goddess, raw gold glimmering in a stream. An exotic bird in a petting zoo. A celebrity among mere mortals.

For the first time, he understood what she'd given up in returning to Marietta. She strode down the catwalk as if born to it. She wore a flowing lavender ankle-length evening gown with a slit that ran halfway up her thigh, revealing one leg and outlining the shape of the other one with every step. Isaac couldn't tear his eyes off her.

She was magnificent.

She was terrifying.

This was not the DeeDee he knew; this was someone destined for greatness.

"DeeDee is wearing an off-the-shoulder raw silk gown designed by Valentino," Logan read from the page, "paired with sling-backs by Jimmy Choo, and highlighted by a Gucci teardrop pendant."

As she passed by their seats, DeeDee gave Isaac a slumberous look. Then she lowered one heavily made-up eye and winked at him. His heart stopped. In that instant, the room disappeared, the lights narrowed, and it was just the two of them, the beauty queen with the heart of gold and the stubborn man with the feet of clay who loved her against his will. Then she looked away. The fragile, fleeting connection was lost.

Hoots of laugher sounded, fingers poking him from behind. "That was for you, Isaac," Austin said.

"DeeDee loves chocolate, yoga, shopping, and telling people what's good for them," Logan finished.

More laughter.

Just then, in Isaac's pocket, DeeDee's cell phone vibrated. He glanced down. He'd promised to keep it safe for her during the show. The number on the screen indicated an out-of-state caller, so he whispered his excuses and quickly slipped to the back of the room to answer it, watching DeeDee at the same time.

"Hello," he said. "Deirdre Cash's phone."

"Who's this?" a male voice snapped. "Never mind. Get me DeeDee."

"Excuse me," Isaac said. "Who's calling?"

"It's Jon. She'll know what it's about. Put her on. Now."

There was an assumption, a possessiveness in this man's voice, that set Isaac's teeth on edge.

He gathered his temper and looked over to the stage. He could see DeeDee showing off her shoes at one end of the runway, waiting for Logan to find his place in the program. "She's occupied."

"With what?" Jon paused. "Who are you?"

"A friend," he answered. "Can I take a message?"

Logan said something and DeeDee bent over at the waist, laughing. She gathered a handful of that elegant dress and sashayed to the other side.

"I've already left her messages. The head of marketing wants to meet her. She's supposed to be here. Where is she?"

Isaac's blood turned to ice. So what that woman, Leda, had said was true. Deirdre was leaving. "She's in Marietta, Montana."

The man on the phone inhaled sharply. The barrage of words that came at him then would have been funny if not for the anger behind them.

Isaac held the phone away from his ear while Jon shouted, trying to make sense of what he was saying. He was DeeDee's agent, apparently. And DeeDee had an appointment in New York.

But if that was true, what was she doing here? Had she mixed up her dates? Forgotten about it in her rush to do the show?

Surely not. But Isaac owed it to her to make sure. No matter how much it hurt.

"Wait a second," Isaac said, interrupting the tirade. "Let me get her for you."

From the back of the room, he waved his hand in the air, hoping to catch her attention without interrupting the show.

"I stuck my neck out for her," Jon said. "It's one thing for her to blow off the nose job, but if she's not on the next plane, I'm done with her."

Nose job? She was considering surgery? Isaac met Dee-Dee's gaze, then lifted the phone and pointed at it. She smiled at him, her eyes shining in the spotlight, and continued pacing while Logan spoke.

"Hang on." He forced himself not to jump to conclusions. "I'm sure it's just a misunderstanding."

After clicking on the flashlight app on DeeDee's phone, he waved it again. He had to let her have her chance, whatever it was.

And if she had to leave, then he had to let her go. Without blame. Look at her, after all. A woman like that deserved the spotlight.

Isaac jumped up and down, causing the people nearest him to look over, frowning.

"Sorry," he muttered.

He pushed his way up to Eric Anders.

"DeeDee's got an important call," he whispered.

"Now?" Eric said, looking horrified.

Isaac nodded. "She needs to take this. Tell her it's New York."

Eric made his way onto the stage and leaned toward Logan, who beckoned to DeeDee.

"Excuse me," she said to the crowd with an exaggerated shrug. "Everything's an emergency."

The audience tittered.

Isaac saw her head jerk when she got the message. Then her back straightened and her expression changed. It happened so quickly he might have imagined it. Surely no one else would have noticed.

But he did.

She looked at him with a soft, sweet smile that made his stomach flop over. Then, very deliberately, she shook her head.

Isaac was confused. She had an opportunity to return to the career of her dreams, and she was giving it up?

DeeDee gave another minute shake of her head.

Isaac lifted the phone again, beckoning, but she only smiled again. This time, he saw sadness. The brittle shine was gone, leaving an open, tender yearning. For what? For him? Dare he hope? Once more, she shook her head and mouthed the word *no*.

"Wait," he whispered to Jon again. He had to be sure.

She had to be sure.

"Sit down," Eric said, none too gently.

Isaac yanked his arm away. "DeeDee," he called. "You want to take this."

DeeDee's eyes widened. "Excuse us," she said with a little laugh. "Somebody's trying to contact me. Since everyone I care about is in this room already, I know it's not important. But my dear friend Isaac is worried. He worries a lot. It's part of what I love about him."

A ripple of laughter rose from the audience. Again, she'd said it so casually, like she loved pizza or old movies. Was she that casual about love?

Or was she saying it again, like this, because he hadn't responded the first time, and she was afraid to confront him?

People were looking at him, waiting for him to sit down so they could continue the show.

He walked closer to the stage. "It's Jon," he said, hating that he was interrupting but desperate for her to understand. If she stayed in Marietta, it had to be by choice. Her choice.

"It's Jon," DeeDee repeated for the crowd. "He's irritated because I refused to get a nose job. What do you think, people? Isn't this nose good enough?"

She tapped the side of her nose again, and the crowd cheered.

"Jon's persistent," she continued, "so I need your help. When I count to three, I want you to join me in saying *Goodbye, Jon*. Can you do that?"

Was she serious? All this time, she'd been wrestling with this huge decision? She knew about her big second chance… and she'd decided not to take it?

I love you and Isaac both, honey.

Was that true?

He spoke into the phone. "Listen hard, Jon. DeeDee has something to say to you." Then he lifted the device.

"One, two, three," DeeDee said, waving her hands like an orchestra conductor.

"Goodbye, Jon!"

The chorus rang out. If the audience was confused, they didn't seem to mind.

Isaac stepped quickly to the back of the room again as the laughter settled and attention turned back to Mark.

"Did you get that?" he asked.

Jon let loose a string of curses. "She's done. You tell her that for me, okay? That's what I get for trying to polish up some rancher's daughter from nowhere—"

Isaac ended the call before he could say something he'd regret. Look at the commitment she'd displayed to Mark, to Cynthia, to Sage and Portia. To the entire town.

To him.

He stood for a moment, breathing hard, his chest thumping.

DeeDee had an opportunity in New York, but she'd turned it down.

She loved him.

THIS, DeeDee thought, *is what matters.* All these people. All these friends.

The show was over. Despite Mark's stumble and Jon's interruption, it was an unqualified success. Donations had flowed in, and everyone had a wonderful time.

And she'd told Isaac, in front of everyone, that she loved him.

Would she ever get a handle on impulse control?

Isaac stood in the corner with Mark, watching while Mark chattered with Sara Maria. Or, more accurately, *to* her. Sara Maria held her arms straight against her sides, but every now and then, she nodded and said something in response.

Why wasn't Isaac coming over to her? Hadn't he heard her?

Maddie's loud laugh rose above the clatter, and DeeDee looked over. Maddie's eyes met hers, as if drawn to her by the same awareness they'd shared as children and then forgotten.

Or maybe only DeeDee had forgotten.

Maddie waved and blew her a congratulatory kiss. She and Mick were folding white tablecloths, moving together, then apart, halving and quartering the unwieldy fabric in a utilitarian, yet intimate, dance.

She'd never seen Maddie so happy.

The entire room was bursting with the joy of a shared endeavor, with community and friendship. So why was her throat so hot and tight? Happy tears, she told herself. That was all.

Nothing to do with Isaac's avoidance. Mark was fine, but DeeDee had pushed him to participate, despite Isaac's wishes. She shouldn't be surprised at Isaac's reaction to Mark's fall. He loved his brother.

Logan Stafford's crew of high school students were busy breaking down the tables and returning them to the storage room. Behind the stage, a crowd of women were slipping clothing onto hangers and shoes into boxes. Children dashed happily between the folding chairs while their parents worked.

Chad and Eric had their heads together at the front of the room, going over the donor sheets. Chad kept a hand on Cynthia, who'd remained in her wheelchair during the entire show, much to DeeDee's relief.

If the mood of the crowd was any reflection on their generosity, this would be the most successful fundraiser to date. A win for Cynthia and CH Solutions. A win for Building Tomorrow. A win for Mark and Sara Maria and their friends. They were part of this community and deserved to be included, not shut away like an embarrassing secret.

DeeDee fingered the tiny scar on her nose. She'd made her choice. Whether Isaac loved her or not, she'd chosen to believe that she was good enough the way she was. Her breath hitched in her chest and she bit her lip to stop it from wobbling.

She'd done this. Pulled it off. She'd made up for her past mistakes with Cynthia. Maybe she could even build a future with Cynthia's company. For real, this time.

Her phone, which had been vibrating like mad for the past half an hour, buzzed again.

Jon… again.

"What now?" she snapped.

"I've got you the perfect gig to resurrect your career and you go MIA?" He paused. "DeeDee, what's wrong with you?"

DeeDee watched Jade and Bob, the black and white Labrador mix who shadowed her every move. Isaac wanted to get Mark a dog. She imagined Isaac jogging through Bramble Park with a golden retriever at his side, an image even more delicious than anything Sage concocted.

She swallowed hard, willing the lump in her throat to go away. At least she had Mr. Fluffy Legs. She'd grown fond of the hideous creature.

"DeeDee!" Desperation rang in Jon's voice. A part of her was sympathetic. He'd no doubt put his own reputation on the line, predicting her response based on his past experiences.

At the back of the room, another figure waved, then gave her the thumbs-up sign. Maya Parrish! She'd managed to come after all. DeeDee waved back, touched by Maya's kindness, grateful that one slate at least had been wiped clean.

All of this felt good. Whatever judgment she'd expected was no more than she deserved, so it was both humbling and freeing to realize that, aside from her family, most people hadn't even registered her absence. But now that she was back, goodwill she'd barely begun earning poured out to her like a waterfall.

"Deirdre Cash!" Jon sounded like he was about to burst a blood vessel. "This is your one and only chance for a come-back. Ignore this and you'll never model again. I'll see to it."

Once upon a time, his power had dazzled her. Jon could open doors for her, get her into the right parties, in front of the right photographers. Now she realized he was little more than an insect, buzzing from flower to flower, always search-ing for his next meal, moving on the moment something better caught his eye, desperate for something, anything, to boost him to the next rung on an endless ladder.

"Do you know how many girls would give their eye teeth to be with me? To have a chance like this? I'm beginning to think I've made a mistake with you."

"You have, Jon. You absolutely have." She laughed. "Thanks for thinking of me and good luck in the future, but I am out."

He screeched something unintelligible, and she held the phone away from her ear.

A rush of warm, sweet air on her neck made her jump.

"Isaac." All the nerve endings along her throat were sing-ing. His breath smelled like chocolate. In his hand, he held a plate of leftover Easter Egg Bark. He didn't look angry.

Without taking her eyes off Isaac, DeeDee lifted the phone back to her face. "Good-bye, Jon," she said. "Don't call again."

She powered off the device and dropped it into her pocket.

Isaac's eyes widened. His jaw dropped. He led her away from the melee, to a quieter corner.

She thought of all the years of denial, the food not eaten, the hours of running to make up for what she did eat, the hunger, the constant fear of not looking good enough, of missing a trend, of becoming obsolete.

She'd tried so hard, yet she'd gotten more satisfaction from running this show for Cynthia than she'd ever had showing off her feet for Dr. Dorne's Corn and Callus Palace. She'd felt better about herself with Isaac and Mark, in jeans and T-shirts, than she ever had in haute couture with Jon.

"I saved some chocolate for you," Isaac said. "I hope you're ready to enjoy it."

"I'm starving," she said.

His eyebrows rose. His dark eyes simmered with heat and longing. Something told her he was offering more than chocolate. Or was that wishful thinking?

"DeeDee, what are you doing?" He stood close, his strong arm braced against the wall behind her, the heat from his body warming her. He could bend down and kiss her and no one would see.

She was suddenly faint and giddy and so full of hope she didn't know if she was going to laugh or cry or start dancing. Or all three.

"I'm done, Isaac." Her voice cracked.

"What happened?" He ran his hand up and down her arm. "We can fix this. How can I help?"

"You don't understand." Laughter bubbled up. There was something wet on her cheeks. "I'm done with New York City. I'm done with modeling."

Isaac cupped her face in his palms. "This is your dream, DeeDee. You can't give up. I don't want you to choose... Marietta... and then spend the rest of your life regretting it."

"No, no," she said.

He wiped a tear from the corner of her eye.

She put her hands over his, stroking his fingers. "Jon kept talking about my big New York comeback... and I believed him. How I only needed to fix a few things about myself, a nose job, some Botox, a little nip here and a tuck there, and I'd be on my way." She shuddered. "I thought that the only way to show people I'd succeeded in life was to do what I said I'd do. You know, local girl makes good. I thought giving up meant I was a failure. But somewhere along the way, I stopped loving it and I didn't even notice. You know, the past few weeks here have been happier than the entire time I spent in the city. Spending time with Mark, with my family, with the friends I didn't even know I had, made me realize that I could have a life here. If I wanted."

She gathered her courage and looked him in the eye. "Do you have something to say to me, Isaac Litton? I've said it twice. It's your turn."

He swallowed. "We've barely known each other a month, DeeDee."

"Five weeks, actually."

Isaac's gaze was impenetrable. "Mark loves you. I don't want him hurt."

It was a fair shot. "I understand. I wouldn't ever hurt him, Isaac."

His eyes narrowed. "What about me? I won't be a consolation prize, DeeDee."

A muscle twitched in his jaw, and she saw how much the words cost him.

"Never," she whispered. "*This* is my comeback, Isaac. I'm home to stay."

His hand shook. His eyes grew shiny as his breathing quickened. "Thank God," he said finally. "DeeDee, I'm so in love with you. All I can think about is kissing you right now, in front of everyone. I hope you don't mind."

"Mind?" She wrapped her arms around his neck. "It's about time, Ike."

And then, finally, his lips were on hers and hope and love and chocolate were all mixed together. It was sweeter than she'd ever imagined.

"Is this what love tastes like?" she murmured against his mouth.

Isaac smiled, pressing his forehead against hers. "Seems to me I've heard that somewhere," he said. "We'll have to do a lot of testing, to be sure."

"Trial and error," she murmured. "I'm up for it."

"Extensive analysis," he responded, nibbling on her bottom lip. "Might take a long, long time."

She looked up, her chest so full it might burst out of her chest. "Oh yeah? How long?"

"Could take forever." He kissed her again. "But let's start with now. You in?"

"Absolutely," she said.

Now was perfect.

Epilogue

Two weeks later

"I CAN'T BELIEVE it." DeeDee looked between her phone and Isaac in amazement.

"Can't believe what?" Isaac said. "Mark, as soon as you're done with your hot chocolate, we have a surprise for you."

They'd stopped in at Copper Mountain Chocolates for their usual treat. Sage always made sure to ask Mark about his exercises before she served him. To date, Mark had lost another three pounds.

"You contacted your clients about donating to the program?" DeeDee pressed a hand to her throat, wanting to laugh and cry and hug Isaac all at the same time.

Chad had just informed her that the final numbers were in. The fundraiser had well exceeded their best-case scenario, thanks to several generous, and unexpected, donations from Chicago-area businesses.

Isaac hadn't even mentioned it.

If she hadn't loved him before…

Isaac shrugged. "Of course. They need write-offs and

prefer causes with a personal connection. It was a no-brainer."

DeeDee leaned over and kissed him, hard. "You are pretty sneaky, Ike. I like that about you."

Chad and Eric had more than they needed to begin the community support program, with Mark as their first client. Logan was already talking about connecting the program with the school system for teenagers with special needs.

And even better, they were in talks with the May Bell Care Home about using a portion of the funds raised to improve their day program—and their staff training. Mrs. Hatcher, upon hearing the news, had promptly given notice, to no one's regret.

DeeDee didn't know exactly what the future held for her, except that she was done with New York. Of all her time in front of cameras and crowds, nothing had brought the high she'd felt when the crowd had cheered for her and Mark.

Cynthia insisted she stay on with CH Solutions, at least until the baby was born, and for the first time, DeeDee believed that the offer was sincere.

Her mom, after meeting Isaac at the show, had been shiny-eyed with delight that her prodigal daughter had not only found herself, but had also found her 'soul mate' as well. Cynthia had scolded her about jinxing it, Norm told her she was jumping the gun, and Maddie informed them all that she'd set them up in the first place.

Sure, the family was meddling. Because they cared.

"Will you be sad to say goodbye?" Isaac asked as they got to their feet.

DeeDee glanced at Mark. "I'll still be seeing plenty of him."

"You could see more of him."

Isaac had been pushing for her to move in with him and Mark, but DeeDee had declined—for now. She still had things to figure out about herself. Since Maddie had finally moved to the lake with Mick, the apartment was hers to sublet.

Her relationship with Isaac was too important for her usual impulsive decision-making process.

As Isaac pulled up in front of the building, pride tugged her shoulders straighter. She couldn't stop smiling. She had her own place, she had a job, and she had friends. She had her family.

She had a great guy.

Make that an *incredible* guy.

Two incredible guys. She loved them both. The same amount, but different kinds, as Mark frequently reminded her.

"Come on, Mark," she said, leading him to the elevator.

When they reached the apartment, she unlocked it and grabbed the can of cat treats she kept by the door.

A gnarly feline ambled around the corner, his moth-eaten tail waving like a flat.

"Mr. Fluffy Legs!" Mark shouted.

He'd been disappointed to learn that his favorite pet had been adopted, and DeeDee had warned Dakota not to tell Mark anything until she'd cleared her plan with Isaac.

"I need a favor, Marco Polo," she said.

"Pay attention, bud," Isaac added. He took DeeDee's hand.

"What?" Mark and the cat were exchanging cheek rubs.

"I need you to look after Mr. Fluffy Legs for me," she said. "At your house."

Mark glanced up at her, his eyes wide. He looked at Isaac.

Isaac grinned and nodded. "He's going to live with us. Is that okay?"

"Yay!" Mark cheered. The cat ran away. "Is DeeDee going to live with us, too?"

DeeDee glared at Isaac. "Did you put him up to that?"

"Hey," Isaac said. "He must have heard someone talking."

"I'm going to live here for a while longer, but Mr. Fluffy Legs will live with you and Isaac. You're going to have to look after him though. Clean his litter box, feed him, brush him. Can you do that?"

Mark nodded solemnly.

"Good." She gave him a soft punch on the shoulder. "Now, go get him and put him in the carrier, okay?"

Mark disappeared after the cat.

"You're amazing, Deirdre Cash." Isaac nuzzled her neck, sending shivers down to her toes.

"I am." She sighed happily. "You're pretty cool, too."

"You free later tonight?" he murmured.

"Always," she replied huskily.

As she said the word, she realized it was true. No matter where she lived now, six months from now, twelve months from now, in this apartment, Isaac's house, or a new place they chose together… she was his.

Forever.

The End

You'll love the next book in…

The Love at the Chocolate Shop series

Love blooms in and around the Copper Mountain Chocolate shop of Marietta, Montana in a twelve book series featuring authors C.J. Carmichael, Melissa McClone, Debra Salonen, Roxanne Snopek, Marin Thomas and Steena Holmes.

Book 1: *Melt My Heart, Cowboy* by C.J. Carmichael

Book 2: *A Thankful Heart* by Melissa McClone

Book 3: *Montana Secret Santa* by Debra Salonen

Book 4: *The Chocolate Cure* by Roxanne Snopek

Book 5: *The Valentine Quest* by Melissa McClone

Book 6: *Charmed by Chocolate* by Steena Holmes

Book 7: *The Chocolate Comeback* by Roxanne Snopek

Book 8: *The Chocolate Touch* by Melissa McClone

Book 9: *Sweet Home Cowboy* by Marin Thomas

Available now at your favorite online retailer!

About the Author

USA TODAY bestselling author Roxanne Snopek writes contemporary romance both sexy and sweet, in small towns, big cities and secluded islands, with families and communities that will warm your heart. Her fictional heroes (like her own real-life hero) are swoon-worthy, uber-responsible, secretly vulnerable and occasionally dough-headed, but animals love them, which makes everything okay. Roxanne writes from British Columbia, Canada, where she is surrounded by wild flowers, wildlife and animals that require regular feeding. She does yoga to stay sane. It works, mostly.

Visit her website at RoxanneSnopek.ca

Thank you for reading

The Chocolate Comeback

If you enjoyed this book, you can find more from all our
great authors at TulePublishing.com, or from your favorite
online retailer.

TULE
PUBLISHING

Made in the USA
Columbia, SC
10 July 2017